Maggie Still Believed In One Man, One Love, One Marriage For A Lifetime.

Part of that dream involved a glorious marriage proposal in which her husband-to-be declared his undying love and devotion.

Never once had she imagined "You're going to have to marry me."

Well, so much for romance, she thought, relegating her dreams to a shadowed corner of her heart. Fantasy had no place in the reality of the moment, the reality of her situation.

But the truth was, she *wanted to marry* J.D.

Dear Reader,

I know you've all been anxiously awaiting the next book from Mary Lynn Baxter—so wait no more. Here it is, the MAN OF THE MONTH, *Tight-Fittin' Jeans*. Mary Lynn's books are known for their sexy heroes and sizzling sensuality...and this sure has both! Read and enjoy.

Every little girl dreams of marrying a handsome prince, but most women get to kiss a lot of toads before they find him. Read how three handsome princes find their very own princesses in Leanne Banks's delightful new miniseries HOW TO CATCH A PRINCESS. The fun begins this month with *The Five-Minute Bride*.

The other books this month are all so wonderful...you won't want to miss any of them! If you like humor, don't miss Maureen Child's *Have Bride, Need Groom*. For blazing drama, there's Sara Orwig's *A Baby for Mommy*. Susan Crosby's *Wedding Fever* provides a touch of dashing suspense. And Judith McWilliams's *Practice Husband* is warmly emotional.

There is something for everyone here at Desire! I hope you enjoy each and every one of these love stories.

Lucia Macro

Senior Editor

Please address questions and book requests to:
Silhouette Reader Service
U.S.: 3010 Walden Ave., P.O. Box 1325, Buffalo, NY 14269
Canadian: P.O. Box 609, Fort Erie, Ont. L2A 5X3

SUSAN CROSBY
WEDDING FEVER

SILHOUETTE *Desire*®
Published by Silhouette Books
America's Publisher of Contemporary Romance

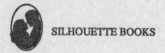

SILHOUETTE BOOKS

ISBN 0-373-76061-2

WEDDING FEVER

Books by Susan Crosby

Silhouette Desire

The Mating Game #888
Almost a Honeymoon #952
Baby Fever #1018
Wedding Fever #1061

SUSAN CROSBY

is fascinated by the special and complex communication of courtship, and so she burrows in her office to dream up warm, strong heroes and good-hearted, self-reliant heroines to satisfy her own love of happy endings.

She and her husband have two grown sons and live in the Central Valley of California. She spent a mere seven and a half years getting through college and finally earned a B.A. in English a few years ago. She has worked as a synchronized swimming instructor, a personnel interviewer at a toy factory and a trucking company manager. Involved for many years behind the scenes in a local community theater, she has made only one stage appearance—as the rear end of a camel! Variety, she says, makes for more interesting novels.

Readers are welcome to write to her at P.O. Box 1836, Lodi, CA 95241.

To Elana, Linda, Robin and Sharon—
my friends and critique partners.
Without you, the fairy tale would have stopped at "Once
upon a time…"

One

J.D. Duran was late. Not by a few "Oh, that's all right" minutes, but by forty-five "How *nice* of you to join us" minutes. He pressed a hand to his jacket pocket, assuring himself the package was there. The package that shouldn't have been necessary. The package that had made him late.

On the surface, the contents of the gold-foil-wrapped box served as a gift for a beautiful woman celebrating her thirtieth birthday. The true purpose, however, went deeper—it could very well save her life, a fact he couldn't share with her.

He left the chill of the San Francisco winter evening behind as he opened a door and entered another world, one of quiet elegance, wealth and status. For a year and a half he'd worked there with few problems, all of them easily managed. Until now.

Pausing at his maître d's podium, J.D. ran a finger down the list of reservations for the night, hoping— No. There he was. Brendan Hastings, the man who lived in a dark, secret world the birthday girl was too innocent to imagine.

J.D. unclenched his fists, touched his pocket again, then headed to the kitchen, mentally inventing excuses for his tardiness. He paused outside the door and listened to the quiet within. Either his normally rowdy co-workers had been struck silent or he was later than he'd realized.

All the excuses he came up with fled his mind the moment he pushed open the door, but he didn't enter. He gripped the door, not letting it close as he saw that the servers' station in the front part of the kitchen was empty—except for her. She faced a stainless-steel barrier that divided the workstation from the cooking area, where the chefs worked in preparation for the dinner crowd, their white hats barely visible above the divider. He traced her rigid spine with his gaze, noted the anger, or irritation, or whatever she was feeling, in the stiffness of her movements. Her shiny coal black hair brushed tensed shoulders as she shuffled items on the worktable. He didn't have to see her bright blue eyes to picture them flashing with emotions, emotions not likely to be either lukewarm or well hidden.

Her voice penetrated the subdued clatter of pots and pans. She was muttering to herself, something about skewering a certain inconsiderate, thinks-he's-God's-gift-to-women maître d'.

He would have smiled if the situation weren't so serious. Instead, he closed his eyes a moment. It wasn't fair to her. Hell, it wasn't fair to *him*. She could only get in the way, probably *would* get in the way. And then what? He didn't need this—either the distraction or the attraction, and she would be suspicious of the changes in him. Then, when the truth came out, she'd hate him for the deception. He wished he had a choice.

Steeling his spine, he stepped into the room.

Maggie Walters pushed her gifts into a pile as she devised a particularly inventive way to punish one of her co-workers—the one who'd been conspicuously absent from her birthday party. Her *thirtieth* birthday, which *everyone* knew was important to her. The others had come to work early to cele-brate—the dishwashers, her fellow waitresses, the bartender, even the manager. But not the maître d'. Not the man she'd most wanted to be there.

"By the time I'm through with him," she muttered, "he'll wish he called in sick."

"Happy birthday, Magnolia."

Maggie's heart danced at the slight inflection that trans-formed her name into a caress. She drew a steadying breath and turned to face the man she'd moments ago threatened with imaginary injury.

James Diego Duran. Tall, dark and handsome didn't begin to describe him. Six foot one inches of sinewy strength, near-black hair with ends that began to curl a few days after each haircut, intelligent dark brown eyes, a killer smile when he chose to use it, and a body that should come with warning labels: Raw Male Within. Approach At Own Risk.

Oh, Lord, he stood before her, stealing her breath, not knowing he was the one she'd wished for earlier when she'd blown out her candles...then just as fervently wished to skewer.

Maggie's anger got swallowed by a sigh. She'd give just about anything to be able to unwrap the tempting package of J.D. Duran, the man of mystery. More than he appeared, cer-tainly; less than her vivid imagination, probably.

Oh, yes, he was one intriguing parcel—and she stood as much chance of getting him for her birthday as Lois Lane did Superman.

Which was a blessing, really, since he didn't show any in-tention of fitting into her long-term plans.

"I'm sorry I missed your party," he said, walking toward her, his eyes steady, assessing.

"No one took attendance." She turned away, attempting to force her thoughts from him by contemplating how she'd get her gifts to the locker room.

Maggie felt his gaze on her for several seconds before he swept by her, passing out of sight. Relaxing, she blew her bangs off her forehead. She really needed to stop drooling over the man. After all, they'd worked together for a year and a half, and seven months ago he'd flatly admitted that he wanted to sleep with her—but wasn't going to.

It could have pulverized a lesser woman's self-confidence. The brief flash of ego she allowed herself made her smile.

He returned with an empty cardboard carton and tossed it onto the table in front of her. "Looks like you need something to carry your presents," he said, taking a beribboned cake knife from her hand and laying it in the box. "This was a gift?"

"Mmm-hmm."

He frowned, then reached for the first item in the pile, a white vinyl photo album. Someone had written Our Wedding in glitter glue across the cover.

"Ah. I had forgotten their plans. A bridal shower," he remarked, casting her a sideways glance as he stood the album on end in the box before holding up two plastic champagne flutes.

She touched one with her fingertip. "Note the beautiful engraving."

Someone had written Maggie on one with a black felt marker and A Prince Among Men on the other. Cocktail straws twined the stems like mutant ribbons. Maggie loved the glasses, as she did all of the silly gifts, even though they represented a not-yet-fulfilled but well-voiced dream.

"Are you sorry now that you broadcasted your deadline of being married by thirty?"

"It was a goal, not a deadline." She lifted her chin. "Besides, I've been a little busy with work and college."

He set a few more items into the box, then stopped and looked at her. "The traditional 'something blue,' I assume," he said.

She looked away from his intense gaze and saw him pick up a small carton of blue condoms, then shift the item back and forth between his hands. Large hands. With long, tapered fingers...and undisguised strength. Her breasts would fit perfectly in his palms. The feel of his rougher skin against her soft flesh would be—

"Subtle bunch we work with."

Startled, she nodded, hearing something different in his voice—a warm huskiness that called to her most basic needs.

He squeezed the carton a moment before arcing it into the box. "I have a gift for you, as well."

"You do?" She frowned at the pleasure he must have heard in her voice. He'd made it clear he didn't want her to flirt with him, or tease him, or do more than have a working relationship only. Which was why she frequently did tease or flirt with him. She recognized the defensive tactic as self-preservation, even if she didn't like herself for doing it.

She dared to look at him and caught his mouth tilting one-sidedly as his eyes softened to liquid chocolate. Why was he looking at her like that? He couldn't turn sociable overnight, could he? Not that he hadn't been friendly before, but this was *friendly.* Man-to-woman friendly.

"I'd like to give you the gift after work," he said. "In private. Maybe at your apartment?"

Okay, do I become pathetically grateful or keep him in suspense? She lifted the cardboard box, giving herself something to do. Pride trickled in, mixed with a little caution. She glanced over her shoulder to where the kitchen crew were busy. "Why not now? We're reasonably alone."

"Humor me, Magnolia."

She held her breath as he reached out and brushed her hair back from her face. His fingertips grazed her cheek. He smiled slowly, devastatingly.

She came out of her stupor, stepping back so fast she knocked over a glass of sparkling cider with her elbow. The cool liquid splattered her calf and dripped into her shoe. "All right, honey, what's goin' on?" she asked, purposefully drawing on her Louisiana accent and the endearment he hated in order to put more than physical distance between them, a tactic she used whenever she felt backed into a corner.

"Nothing."

Letting her raised eyebrows show her disbelief, she dropped the box on the counter and kicked off her shoe. He pulled a white handkerchief from his back pocket, crouching as she did.

"I'm capable of cleaning my own foot, thank you." She snatched the cloth from his hand, afraid to let him touch her again, annoyed that he was so prepared. She didn't know any men who carried handkerchiefs anymore. "You're playin' some kinda game with me. I don't like it."

"You didn't care for the gift I gave you last year. I am trying to improve this year," he said as they stood in unison.

"Right."

"I have always been truthful with you, Magnolia."

That made her hesitate. He had, in fact, been so honest it had hurt sometimes, and in her more generous moments, she admired him for never ducking the truth. She stared at her foot. Lord, she was tired of hiding her feelings for him behind flirtatious antagonism. Just once she'd like for them both to be completely honest.

She dropped the handkerchief into her carton of gifts before hugging the box to her, still wondering why he was acting different.

She looked at him. "All right. After work at my place."

"You could say that as if you looked forward to it just a little," he said, plucking his damp handkerchief from the box and balling it into his fist.

Maggie pursed her lips. The possibilities for a pleasant evening seemed slim to none at this point. Maybe the risk was too great, after all. "Look, Diego, we'll only fight if we get together later. You know we will."

"We don't fight. We just don't agree on much."

"On anything."

"I think if we try, we can find some common ground, Magnolia."

"Somehow I doubt it could include conversation."

He smiled then, that smile that pierced her lungs and let all the air out.

"This should be fascinating," she commented as she leaned into the door and left.

J.D. watched the door swing shut, his smile fading. In his mind he heard her call him by his middle name again, drawing it out, emphasizing her exclusive use of it—just as he was the only one to call her Magnolia.

Magnolia. Her mother hadn't named her well. She was no pale, fragile blossom who wilted easily....

He roused himself to clean the workstation, and greet the chefs, then he left the kitchen to assume his post as maître d' of the Casola, an exclusive club housed in a converted Victorian mansion in the heart of San Francisco. The forty-year-old private club offered peace and privacy to the famous and the infamous as they socialized in an environment free of paparazzi and curious onlookers.

He glanced into the elegantly furnished dining room. Maggie moved from table to table lighting candles, her crisp white shirt reflecting light and shadows from the flames, her fitted black skirt hinting at graceful feminine curves—a narrow waist and an appealing flare of hips. Her usual thin black tie had been replaced by one that was red and dotted with tiny gold angels. She hummed somewhat on-key with Bing as he dreamed of a white Christmas. Personally, J.D. was grateful there were just a couple of days left to endure the Christmas music filtering through well-placed speakers. All that good cheer. If the members knew what really went on here...

Taking the stairs two at a time, he checked each of the card rooms and billiard rooms on the second floor, as was his routine. A quick detour into the gender-segregated lounges assured him all was in order.

He hurried downstairs to take his position at the podium fifteen feet from the front door. His eyes focused on the name that stood out as though written in blood-red. Brendan Hastings. How could such a simple name impact so many lives?

After eight years of doing the same job Tuesday through Saturday nights, Maggie functioned by rote—which was a good thing, since her mind wasn't anywhere near work tonight. Instead she spun imaginative scenarios of possibilities for her meeting with Diego, from the argument that would most likely occur to an improbable moment of passion.

At least indifference wouldn't be a likelihood. Their relationship tended to cling to the ends of the scale, at either barely controlled irritation or barely controlled desire, never balanced at its midpoint. She'd gotten used to the extremes and even kind of liked it that way.

Except she had a feeling that in just about an hour everything was going to change.

She put on a smile as she focused on her customer, an attractive man in his late forties. "Here you are, Mr. Hastings. Your favorite. Chocolate cheesecake and espresso."

His companion ate nothing, his job apparently only to take notes, not to do anything as mundane as indulge in dessert. She wondered about the demanding man who kept his employees working this late, something he'd done from the first night he'd come to the Carola the week before.

"Ahh, thank you, Maggie. Did I get the last slice?"

"I saved it just for you. I know it's the only dessert on the menu that tempts you."

"Excellent. It's important to give in to what tempts us, don't you think?"

"I think dessert's one of life's little pleasures."

"What tempts *you?*" Brendan asked, his tone of voice provocative.

"I'm mighty partial to peach pie." Suddenly uncomfortable, she let her drawl thicken, although she left off the "honey" she generally added when speaking with her familiar customers.

She knew she still had to face the signing of the check, which he did with great ceremony, first scrawling his signature across the bill in handwriting as legible as the Richter reading of an earthquake, then tucking a tip into her skirt pocket as he left. Many customers had their quirks about how they paid bills. She hadn't thought too much of it, at least, not after that first time, when she'd been so startled by his familiarity—and she'd had dishes in each hand. She would have complained except that his hand never lingered, neither did he make suggestive remarks. However...something was different tonight.

First, Diego; now, this man. She wondered if there was a full moon.

"Excuse me," she said, escaping with a polite smile. "I'll go tell J.D. your request."

As she left his table she considered Brendan Hastings and how perfect he appeared. She couldn't imagine his dark blond hair messed up—ever—as if it might constitute a crime against nature. The rest of him was just as untouchable. Cool gray eyes, strong nose, sharp cheekbones, a solid, muscular body. His clothing was European, from his tailored London suits to his handmade Italian shoes. His diamond pinky ring flashed brilliantly in the candlelight.

All in all, he was an elegant man. Just not her type.

"Stop scowlin', honey," Maggie said as she came up beside Diego, provoking him, keeping tension between them. "You'll freeze your face like that."

"Another of Mama's homespun homilies, Magnolia?"

Maggie almost sighed. She loved the look of him in his tuxedo, which emphasized his long, lean lines and superb posture. Just the way he'd angled his head her way without turning his body made every cell in her body play leapfrog for a few seconds.

"Mr. Hastings wants to reserve a card room for tomorrow night," she said, finally taking care of the business that had sent her Diego's way.

He inclined his head to Brendan, who she noted was watching them without expression, then Diego turned on his heel, leaving Maggie to frown after him. She'd never seen him react to any guest as he had to Brendan. The nod Diego had given him should have been deferential. It had come across as regal. Of course, Diego had never acted like any other maître d' she'd worked with.

She moved on to another table. "How was your meal?" she asked Misty Champion as she cleared the dishes.

The president of Misty Nights Lingerie and her current remedy for holding middle age at bay—young, blond and studly—had come in for a late dinner. Her escort was gone, probably sent to call and wait for her chauffeur, part of Misty's own quirky bill-paying ritual. She never let her escort watch her pay the check.

"Dinner was perfect, as usual. What do you think of Joseph?"

"Stunning."

Misty laughed, the smoky sound carrying in the near-empty room so that Brendan turned their direction. He eyed Misty until she lifted her almost-empty wineglass and toasted him before draining it. Maggie glanced away, not watching his reaction, afraid he might decide she cared.

"Stunning and not overly bright," Misty said of Joseph as she dabbed her mouth with her napkin. "Unlike the man who has been eyeing you like a Christmas present." She stood, sweeping a beautifully wrapped package off the seat beside her and setting it on the table. "Happy birthday, hon. I designed this with you in mind. Promise you'll wear it the second time you sleep with him."

Him? Maggie hoped she was talking about Diego, but was afraid she meant Brendan. "Um, the second time?"

"The first time will be spontaneous, of course. Fiery." Her eyes glazed a moment. "The second will be different."

"Do you have someone in mind for me, Misty?"

"The same man you have in mind, I suspect. I hear he likes red."

Before Maggie could respond, Diego appeared with Misty's silver fox coat and helped her into it.

"Thank you, Mr. Duran."

"You're welcome, Ms. Champion."

Maggie reacted to the surprising intimacy in their voices, implying a relationship she'd never before considered. Misty liked men at least twenty years younger than her forty-five years. At thirty-two, Diego missed the mark by seven years. Had they been lovers? She looked from one to the other, observing their subtle smiles, as if each knew a secret.

"May I escort you to the door?" Diego asked Misty.

"In a minute. I need to speak to someone first."

"Thank you for the birthday present," Maggie said.

"My pleasure, hon. How's the design coming?"

"I'll have the sample ready in a couple of days. It's very romantic."

"Romantic. Well, there's a first time for everything. My buyers will be shocked." She winked at Maggie as she glided by, then came up beside Brendan and bent to whisper something in his ear.

"Are you working with Misty?" Diego asked Maggie as they waited, glued to the scene like onlookers at an accident.

"Um, I had an idea for a new product for her line—a departure from her usual stuff. What do you suppose she's saying to him?"

"I'd like to know," he said. "It's an interesting combination, don't you think? She would eat him alive."

"I don't know. I think he's used to getting what he wants."

He cast her a cool glance. "Has he been bothering you, Magnolia?"

Why, he's jealous, she realized, his tone of voice saying more than his words. How intriguing. How very intriguing. "These plates are getting heavy."

J.D. watched her walk away, then he mentally shook his head as Misty strolled back, her hips swaying provocatively, and accepted his escort from the room.

"Thanks again for the other night," she said, her husky voice full of emotion.

"My pleasure."

"I'm not too sure about that. But you saved my life. I won't forget it."

"Right time, right place," he said with a shrug. "Quit hanging around those kinds of bars, Misty. Trouble's the only thing you're going to find."

"Which begs the question of why you were there, doesn't it?" She sighed. "Sometimes I just need to be where no one knows or cares who I am."

He heard the loneliness in her voice. He, too, lived a lonely life, although for very different reasons. His was a loneliness that meant safety for those he cared about.

"Where'd you go, lover?" Misty asked J.D. as they reached the door of the club.

He smiled at her. "Not far."

"Are you sure I can't repay you with a little more than thanks?"

"I make it a rule to avoid personal business with guests."

She fingered his lapel. "You don't break rules, I suppose."

"Not personal ones."

"An interesting answer."

"If I had accepted you, you'd be backpedaling your way out of it right now. You and I both know there's someone more than willing to end your loneliness, Misty."

"We've sung this tune before." Her blond Adonis opened the door behind her. "Good night, then. Oh, J.D.? I did remember red's your favorite color."

He puzzled over her words as the door closed on her rich laugh. Returning to the dining room, he observed Hastings slipping something into Maggie's skirt pocket.

"Thank you for joining us tonight," J.D. said as he came up beside them.

Hastings's irritation at the interruption was hardly noticeable, only a slight twitch of his left eye.

J.D. didn't question what intrigued the man. Magnolia possessed a lethal combination of beauty, energy and sensuality that she didn't seem aware of, making her even more attractive. If asked, she'd probably call herself a pretty good flirt. And certainly she possessed a kind of wholesomeness that kept most men at flirtation distance, the place she'd established for guests and members of the Carola, no matter how famous, how powerful or how insistent they were.

She moved in and out of roles as situations warranted, a

skill he admired, even though it often meant she played a role with him, as well.

"I'll see you tomorrow night," Hastings said.

"Good night, sir," she said.

"I'll clear the table while you change," J.D. said after Hastings left.

She looked at him, surprised. "A lofty maître d' would sink so low as to clear a table?"

"I thought perhaps you'd be tired. After all, you're thirty now. Old. Your stamina must be fading."

Maggie responded to his teasing by crossing her arms and cocking a hip. She looked around, making sure they were alone. "I can finish my work here, jog home and still have enough energy to make love, honey. I'm in my prime."

She shivered as he ran a finger along her jaw. Fog crept into her brain, masking logical thought.

"What did Hastings put in your pocket?" he asked so softly she had to lean toward him to hear the whole sentence.

"Huh?"

"Hastings. Did he give you money?"

The synapses in her brain started transmitting information again.

"Of course he gave me money," she said as she turned and picked up the dirty dishes. "A tip. You know, this hot-and-cold business of yours is really gettin' on my nerves."

"How much of a tip?"

"None of your business."

He slid a hand into her skirt pocket, shocking her. The cup rattled against the saucer in her right hand; in her left, the fork slid off the dessert plate. The feel of his hand against her hip, however briefly, brought forth all sorts of images that danced before her eyes, then faded into confusion over whether he was establishing a closer relationship with her or preventing her from having one with someone else.

"What are you doing?" She tried to jerk away. He held her in place as he drew the folded currency from her pocket and turned it to look at its value.

"*Dios.* A hundred dollar bill, Magnolia?"

She stared in amazement. Brendan always left her a generous tip, but this was staggering. She swallowed. "I give good service."

He unfolded the bill, revealing a white business card with a phone number handwritten on the back. He held it close to her face for her to read, front and back.

She looked from the card to him. "At least he didn't write, 'There's more where this came from.'"

"It is implied."

"I'm not stupid, honey. I know what it means."

"Do not call me 'honey.' You use your Southernness like a shield, when it is convenient. I am serious here."

"You think you don't fall back on your background, as well? Listen to yourself. *Do not. It is. I am.* And your machismo gets pretty tiresome, too. You don't have the right to tell me what to do. But that's been your choice all this time, not mine, as you well know." She angled her right hip his way. "Return my property, please."

Holding her captive with his dark, unblinking gaze, he deliberately tucked the card and money into the breast pocket of her shirt. She held her breath as he stuffed them to the bottom, the backs of his fingers more than lightly grazing her nipple, which pebbled at the first touch of his fingers and ached as he pulled his hand away.

She fought for every ounce of control she could muster. "If you're done manhandling me…?"

J.D. jammed his hands in his pockets. "I cannot—*can't* help the way I speak. I didn't learn English until I was an adult."

"Don't be idiotic. I love the way you talk."

The words were tossed over her shoulder as she stormed off, leaving behind a breeze scented with perfume and Magnolia.

He cursed himself with each stride she took. He needed her to appear unattainable in Hastings's eyes. To do that, J.D. had to have her attention focused on him. He was just looking out for her—

So what was that adolescent move to grab a quick feel? he asked himself. Machismo, as she called it? Wish fulfillment? Long-denied need? All three?

He didn't change his clothes, instead leaned against the wall and waited her out. She finally emerged from the women's locker room dressed in blue jeans and a sweatshirt proclaiming English Majors Are Novel Lovers. She carried her carton of presents, the still-wrapped box from Misty balanced on top.

"I parked a couple of blocks behind you," he said. "I'll meet you at your apartment."

"You know where I live?" She tipped her head to one side. "How come I've known you all this time and I hardly know anything about you?"

"Maybe it's time to find out."

"Maybe it is."

They walked silently to their cars. As she drove off, he started his engine and put the car in gear, then he noticed a dark sedan pull away from the curb a hundred feet ahead. He'd learned to trust his instincts, so he tailed the sedan that slowed to almost a complete stop when Maggie pulled into the garage below the duplex she rented.

He followed the car until it disappeared into the valet parking area of the expensive hotel where Hastings rented the penthouse.

J.D. stopped at a pay phone and punched in a familiar number. "I'm sorry to wake you, boss," he said in greeting.

"No problem. What's up?"

He glanced around as he heard Callahan yawn. "He wants to deal tomorrow night."

"We'll cover you."

"Okay. See you."

"Wait a second, J.D. Did you give it to her?"

"Not yet."

"Are you sure you don't want to bring her in on it? If she'd go out with him—"

Creative Spanish epithets peppered the air within the phone booth.

"Lighten up, pal. I was kidding."

"Don't kid with me about Magnolia."

"You'll relax after you give it to her."

"I don't trust it," J.D. said.

"Hey, it's state of the art."

"Yeah. *Experimental* state of the art."

"So, figure out a backup."

He glanced at his watch. Too much time had passed. "Already got it covered."

"I figured as much. Relax already."

"When this is over. Maybe."

Two

Maggie eyed her mantel clock when it chimed once, a delicate *ping* that pierced her anticipation. Twelve-thirty. He should have been at her apartment twenty minutes ago.

She leaned forward on the sofa, resting her elbows on her thighs as she stared at the crystal bowl mounded with shimmering Christmas ornaments that sat on her coffee table. She had to face facts. He wasn't coming.

She wasn't surprised. Not really. He'd changed his mind. Probably decided it wasn't worth spending time with someone who goaded him into an argument whenever he got close. They were so different, she knew they'd never have a serious relationship. What they really needed was to sleep together, to satisfy their curiosity, then the source of antagonism that hovered constantly would be wiped out forever.

Not here, though. They should go to his place. Better yet, to a hotel. Some neutral location where memories wouldn't linger and taunt.

Spoken like a woman of experience, Magnolia Jean. She

pushed her hair away from her face, then let it fall again. The sum total of her experience with the opposite sex wouldn't constitute three pages in her autobiography, *if* she included her fourth-grade crush on Bobby Don Morgan. But she'd imagined making love with Diego so many times, she had choreographed the experience detail by detail. At least, what she would do to *him.*

Before he'd come into her life, she'd dated at least, hoping to meet her lifetime partner. But in the past year, she'd hardly gone out at all, finding flaws in every man who invited her, even though the word *thirty* seemed lit in neon across her forehead each time she looked in her bathroom mirror.

Thirty. Where had the time gone? She couldn't wait much longer, didn't have the luxury to deal with the attraction to Diego and still get started on a family before she was any older—as old as her mother had been.

The quiet tapping on her front door sent an avalanche of reaction tumbling over her. Boulders of relief, followed by pebbles of annoyance. She counted to ten, then opened the door. Desire rebuilt the mountain instantly. She resented it as much as she welcomed it.

"I figured you changed your mind." Maggie feigned a yawn as she turned away, letting him close the door himself.

"I'm sorry. I was detained by a...by a— Did *you* decorate this, Magnolia?"

She turned around. Diego stood, his hands in his pockets, surveying her living room.

"Every bit of it." Was that a look of shock or wonder? She knew her voice held an edge of defensiveness, as if daring him to comment unfavorably. She glanced around the room with its framed counted cross-stitch samplers and groupings of baskets and candles and photographs. Pristine eyelet fabric draped small round tables on which Tiffany lamps glowed, the yellow and blue glass reflecting the dominant colors of the room, even competing with the Christmas tree lights as they were.

"It's a little crowded with all the holiday decorations," she said as he moved around the room, inspecting without commenting. He picked up a heart-shaped pillow and it struck her how utterly feminine it—everything—was. Frilly, romantic, old-fashioned. Or maybe it was just that he was so very masculine.

"What color do you call this?" he asked, breaking the silence.

"Robin's egg blue." She watched him replace the pillow slightly askew, resisted the temptation to march over and straighten it.

"It matches your eyes."

J.D. tried to align the overall impression of her home with his deep-seated image of her. He'd always thought of her as a contemporary woman, a feminist. Certainly, her sassy mouth was pure nineties. If he'd even once tried to picture the environment she lived in, he would have imagined white and chrome and glass, something modern and sleek, certainly nothing close to this...this Suzy Homemaker vision.

Except, of course, he'd known about the fund she'd been adding to for years, saving for the wedding gown of her dreams. Everyone at the Carola knew about it. But no one knew why the gown or the age-thirty goal was so important, except probably her sister, Jasmine.

"Would you like some wine, Diego? And I've got cheese and crackers, as well." She didn't wait for his reply but headed toward the kitchen. "Take off your jacket. Get comfortable."

"Magnolia."

She turned around, her brows lifted in inquiry.

"Come here, please."

"Why?"

He chuckled. "You are so suspicious."

"Well, honey, you're behavin' awfully different tonight."

"Am I?" He ignored her Southern belle routine, and took the necessary steps to bridge the gap. "I'm trying to find a way to communicate with you without arguing."

From his pocket he pulled out the gold-foil-wrapped box and pressed it into her right hand. She hefted it lightly.

"Hmm. Smaller than last year's oh-so-personal engraved pen and pencil set."

"Haven't you forgiven me for that yet?"

She tossed it once, caught it cleanly. "Heavy for its size, though. Professionally wrapped."

"You're worth it."

"Probably offered free gift wrapping with purchase," she said, casting him a quick glance before holding the package at eye level and examining it further. "Could be a key chain."

"Monogrammed," he offered.

"I'd accept nothing less." She shook it, holding it close to her ear. "A box within a box."

"You're good at this."

"When I was growing up I guessed all of my Christmas presents before I opened them."

"You were never surprised?"

She made a sound of disgust. "My mother was predictable."

He leaned close. "Why don't you just open it?"

"But then the anticipation ends." Maggie held her breath as she savored his nearness and warmth, and the scent she'd recognize anywhere.

He dipped his head a little farther. His breath stirred her bangs. "Open it."

He'd taken off his tie and unfastened the top button of his shirt before he'd arrived. Maggie's nose was an inch from the open vee of his pleated shirt. Her teenaged niece had once pronounced him a—

"Stud," she sighed.

"What?"

She stepped back. "Uh, stud. Your stud's loose." She tucked the present under her chin and slid a hand behind his shirt to fiddle with the black onyx and gold stud. The backs of her fingers brushed chest hair. The moment froze in time until she felt his hands encircle her wrists and move her back.

He pulled the gift from under her chin, placed it wordlessly in her hand.

Maggie swallowed. She peeled off the pretty wrappings and tipped a burgundy velvet container out of a box bearing the discreet emblem of Rappaport Jewelers. The hinge didn't make even the tiniest creak as she pushed up the velvety lid. Her hand hovered over the contents. "Why, it's beautiful!"

She sought Diego, confusion swamping her. The gift was personal and expensive—a sparkling chain bearing a heavy gold pendant shaped like a teardrop, perhaps an inch long and half an inch wide at the base.

"May I?" he asked, extending his hand. "Turn around. Tip your head forward."

She waited what seemed like an hour before he lifted the chain over her head. As he fastened the clasp, his fingertips grazed her neck, enough to make her skin prickle, but not enough to call it seduction. The pendant itself rested at heart level. She turned around to thank him.

"I wish I'd changed into something nicer. Something silk to show it off," she said, looking down, lifting a hand toward it.

He touched three fingers to the pendant as it nestled at a level just above the front clasp of her bra. His thumb and little finger grazed the inner curve of her breasts. Their gazes connected; her hand fell away.

Where did he come from, this James Diego Duran, who admitted he desired her, yet resisted her so easily; who avoided touching her for a year and a half, then the first time he did, touched her intimately? Oh, she knew of his background, of his difficult childhood, but that didn't explain the man, only some of the reasons why he behaved as he did sometimes.

"The necklace is all right?" he asked as he pulled his hand back.

"It's incredible."

"You won't ever take it off?"

"Ever?"

"You won't shove it in a drawer if you get angry at me?"

"It'd spend more time in my drawer than around my neck."
She smiled at him until he smiled back. "How about some
wine now?"

He hesitated. "I should leave."

They continued to stare at each other.

She inched closer. "Would you like to see what Misty designed for my birthday?"

"Probably not."

She smiled. "It's just a little something—"

"I'm sure it is. I've seen catalogs of her products."

"Well, I love it, of course," she drawled. "But I'd like a
man's opinion."

Frozen, J.D. watched her stroll across the room and lift up
a box lid. She withdrew a teddy fashioned of red satin and
lace, and dangled it by the straps as she moseyed back to him.

Dios. He recognized the design of the garment, if not the
garment itself. After he'd rescued Misty from those dirtbags
the other night, he'd driven her home. She'd asked him what
his ideal woman wore to entice him. "Just her skin," he'd
replied. When she hadn't accepted that as an answer, he'd
described the frothy bit of nothing Magnolia was holding in
front of her as though she didn't think he could imagine her
clothes stripped away and the red see-through concoction
molding her enticing curves.

"Misty's quite a talented designer, isn't she?" Maggie
asked, stretching the bra cups at the sides until they settled
provocatively over her.

"It suits you."

"Does it? I tend to favor pastel colors in my lingerie. You
think red is suitable with my coloring?"

"You think men think about things like that?"

She was quiet a moment, then said, "If you were going to
buy this for...a woman, what would make you decide to purchase it?" Her voice had dropped an octave; her eyes took on
a sleepy, sexy look.

He fingered the lace at the bodice. "I would wonder if it's
low enough to expose her breasts almost all the way, so there's

a danger of them spilling out if she breathes deep. I'd want her nipples visible through the lace. I'd wonder how easily it comes off. I'd want it not to be fragile, so that I don't have to be too careful or too controlled when I take it off her.'' He slid his hand down the fabric, down her, to toy with the snaps at the crotch. "I would want the fabric thin enough to feel how wet she gets when I touch her.''

"You want a lot," she said, her voice catching breathlessly on her imagination.

"Oh, yes.''

"I could go slip this on…''

He held her gaze a few seconds, then he bent slowly toward her and brushed a fleeting kiss against her cheek.

Waves of sensation rolled through her. She forgot to breathe. When she did take in air again, he was gone, along with the unexpected pleasure he'd brought that suddenly burst like a birthday balloon when the door clicked shut, leaving her alone and bewildered.

Needing to analyze what had just happened, she paced her living room, walking off excess energy. She wasn't completely sure of his intentions after tonight, but he seemed to be wanting a deeper relationship. When the phone rang a few minutes later, she snatched up the receiver and said hello.

"I forgot to say good-night.''

Diego. She dropped onto the sofa and tucked her legs under her. "Are you home already?''

"I'm in my car. I'll be home in about ten minutes.''

"I'm already in bed," she said languidly, as if stretching out on satin sheets. "Naked, except for your necklace.''

She smiled at the long pause on the other end.

"Are you?'' he asked finally.

"No. But I thought you might like to imagine it.''

He didn't answer.

"Why the sudden interest, Diego?''

"I have always been interested in you, Magnolia.''

She closed her eyes, enjoying the way his slight accent turned her name into an endearment that sent ripples of pleasure down her spine. She loved the remnants of his half-Mexican heritage. He, on the other hand, tried very hard to leave it behind.

"I apologize for what happened," he said into the silence. "I shouldn't have...teased like that."

"There's something between us, Diego. It's getting harder and harder to ignore."

"I know."

"We need to deal with it sometime."

"We work together. We have to be careful of how we deal with it."

"I'm not asking for marriage," she said, not wanting to examine her words further. "I'm looking to end the tension."

When he didn't respond, she said good-night and hung up, letting him off the hook.

J.D. pushed the button to disconnect the call. He closed his eyes a moment as he waited for the traffic light to turn green. Naked, except for his necklace. *Dios.* After he locked in the image, he smiled. She was paying him back for the way he'd teased her. That's why he hadn't ever given her the slightest encouragement. She was too smart, too quick. Too addictive. Too much woman.

They had their differences. She planned everything; he liked just to react. She organized her life to the minute; he'd rather be spontaneous. She was an open book; he was locked tight as a diary.

He wished for both their sakes that he could have kept the distance that he'd established and held all this time, but he couldn't. No matter how much she would hate him afterward.

He glanced at the dashboard clock. Making sure he wasn't followed, he drove across the Golden Gate Bridge, then maneuvered the twists and turns of Highway 101 and Sausalito until he pulled into the driveway of a small house guarded by an abundance of winter-hardy foliage. A light burned from his father's office. Relieved, he let out a breath. His father was the only person in the world he could talk to about Magnolia *and* his job. He pictured him, relaxed in his high-backed leather chair, listening, advising, encouraging, so different from his mother, the mother he had seen only once in the past fourteen years. "Jimmy," he'd say, followed by words of wisdom. He wished for the thousandth time he'd known his father during his childhood.

But that was history.

Her Christmas presents were wrapped. Her new winter coat needed only to have the buttons sewn on. She had time to spend on the magazine article for which she had a January 13 deadline. She booted her computer and opened the file for her final article in a series of fifteen she'd been contracted to write for *A Woman's Life* on organizing busy lives. "Creating storage space where there is none," she read at the top of the screen. "An organized home reduces stress—"

Maggie stopped typing as she cocked an ear toward her front door. Someone had knocked. She hurried into the living room. "Who is it?"

"Delivery for Miss Walters."

She opened the door an inch. A young woman stood there, holding an elegant arrangement of long-stemmed white roses in a crystal vase.

"Oh, how beautiful," she exclaimed, pushing the door open and reaching for them. Diego's intentions really were serious.

She shut the door and set the vase in the center of her dining room table, inhaling the sweet rose fragrance as she reached for the tiny white envelope.

Smiling, she pulled out the card. *I will make thee beds of roses. BH.*

BH? Brendan, not Diego? And he was quoting Christopher Marlowe, Maggie realized, horrified—"The Passionate Shepherd to His Love," until now, one of her favorite poems. She couldn't remember telling him she was an English major, but maybe she had. Or was he just trying to impress her with his knowledge?

How had he found out where she lived? Certainly no one

at the Carola would have divulged it. Had he followed her home? Repulsed by the thought, she rubbed the chill from her arms as she walked to her front window and looked out. No limousine, no stranger leaning against the lamppost across the street, nothing out of the ordinary.

The phone rang, startling her.

"Good morning, Maggie."

Brendan. "Who is this?"

A soft chuckle preceded his words. "I was disappointed that you didn't call me. Did you get my flowers?"

She continued to play dumb. "Mr. Hastings?" Silence. She sighed inwardly. There was no way she would win any battle of wits with this man. "They're lovely, but I must ask you not to send me anything ever again. I can't accept gifts from you."

"You deserve lovely things."

"I don't lack for anything. I like my life just as it is. I have plenty for my needs."

"'The lady doth protest too much, methinks.'"

The man quotes Shakespeare—accurately, no less. "I'm being honest with you. I don't want you to call me or send me gifts."

"I do so like the chase, Miss Walters."

"I'm not teasing you, sir. And I'm involved with someone."

He laughed. "Sir? Am I that much older than you? I just wanted you to know I'll be out of town through the holidays. I'll call you when I get back."

"Didn't you reserve a card room for tonight?"

"Cancel it for me, will you? Oh, and Maggie? I happen to know there's no one special in your life right now."

She stared at the receiver long after it went dead. Hanging it up quietly, she thought about how much he knew about her. She eyed her front door, double-checking that it was locked.

If Maggie had any doubt that Diego's interest was tied to Brendan's, that doubt was erased during the next week. Now that Brendan was gone, Diego once again wore calmness and control like his elegant tuxedo. She was not only irritated, but discouraged. And suspicious again of the reason for his sudden focus on her. She'd thought their relationship had taken a positive turn on her birthday, but he hadn't even accepted her invitation to share Christmas with her.

Still, she wore the necklace. And she didn't miss the fact he always checked that she did, even though he never commented on it.

She wondered what he'd do if he knew Brendan was sending her gifts.

The packages that arrived almost daily didn't tempt her, but she was curious about the cards and always opened them. The first one read, *A gown made of the finest wool. BH.* Still quoting Marlowe. That was followed a couple of days later by *Fair lined slippers for the cold. BH.* And then, *A belt of straw and ivy buds, with coral clasps and amber studs. BH.*

Because she knew the poem so well, she knew where he was headed with his gifts. The payoff came on New Year's Eve late in the afternoon, when a small box was delivered to which a card had been attached—*Come live with me, and be my love. BH.*

She shook the box, speculating on the contents. The others had been so easy. This one could be anything. Jewelry, maybe. Brendan would definitely go the ostentatious route, advertising how much in material goods he could offer her. Or perhaps it was a house key. Solid gold, of course, and diamond studded. She was smiling at the thought when the phone rang and she said hello.

"Magnolia."

"Well, well. James Diego Duran." She dropped onto the sofa. "To what do I owe the honor of a communication from you?"

A slight pause. "Did I interrupt something?"

"Nope."

"Have you been sampling New Year's champagne early?" She grinned. "Nope. High on life."

"Why?"

"I was just sitting here pondering absurdities."

"Such as?"

"Ohhh, such as…roses in winter. Solid gold, diamond-studded house keys. People who can quote Shakespeare accurately."

"These things are absurd to you?"

"You don't find solid gold, diamond-studded house keys absurd?"

"I suppose so. Are you in possession of one?"

"Not yet." She smiled at the ceiling as she contemplated his silence. He wanted to ask. Oh, how he wanted to ask. But she'd bet her life's savings he wouldn't.

"I called for a reason, Magnolia."

"Of course you called for a reason, honey. You never do anything without a reason." *And I'd really like to know why you teased me the other night and have ignored me ever since.*

His pause was short but meaningful. Was he counting to ten?

"I wanted to know if you would celebrate New Year's with me tonight," he said.

Out of character. Definitely out of character. What was going on? She swooped up the phone base and carried it with her as she paced her living room. "Well, thank you so much, honey, for believin' I would be free on New Year's Eve."

"*Are* you busy?"

"As a matter of fact, I am. My date will be here momentarily and I still have to get dressed." She glanced at the clock. Her nephew, Matthew, was due to stop by on his way home from a friend's house nearby, and Maggie would drive them both to her sister's house. She could have canceled with Jasmine and her family for the night, of course, but she wouldn't give Diego the satisfaction, not after ignoring her all week. "I can't believe you waited until now to ask."

"I hadn't expected to be free," he said.

"Your date backed out, huh?"

"That's not what I meant. I'm sorry if I offended you. Who are you going out with?"

"Someone tall, blond and handsome who asked me very early to make sure I'd be free. So, next time, make me more than an afterthought, will you, honey? Bye."

"Magnolia?"

"*What?*"

"I can quote Shakespeare, if it means so much to you."

"This I've gotta hear."

"'A horse! a horse! my kingdom for a horse!'"

A short, surprised laugh burst from her as she heard the line go dead. With any luck, he'd see through her ploy and call her back. And maybe she would go out with him, after all.

She set down the telephone, then hurried into her bedroom to dress. Ten minutes later, a knock sounded on her door.

"Coming," she called, teetering on one black satin high heel as she jammed on the other one. She scooped up three-inch-long rhinestone earrings and fastened them on as she moved from her bedroom into the living room. She stopped at the front door, settled her clingy black dress down so that the hem was its normal five inches above her knees, then turned the knob, expecting to greet her nephew.

Two defensive linemen loomed in her doorway. The larger of the two, the one minus a neck, thrust a bouquet of white roses straight at her and let go, forcing her to catch it.

"There's a card," he mumbled, his granite jaw barely moving.

Maggie eyed the flowers, then the men. From Brendan, of course. To appease Tweedledee and Tweedledum, who stood with their feet apart and legs locked to support their bulk, she plucked the envelope from inside the cellophane wrapping, then set the bouquet aside and opened the card—*An unforgettable evening awaits you—as do I, eagerly. BH.*

With her hand on the door, ready to shut it, she said, "Please inform Mr. Hastings that I have other plans."

Tweedledee and Tweedledum exchanged glances. Dee cleared his throat. "We can't leave without you."

Something trickled down her spine. "You most certainly may. *I have other plans.*"

Before she could close the door, Dum slammed his arm against it. She heard wood splinter a second before they barged into her apartment, pulling her along as they went, somehow shutting the door behind them. Everything happened in one fluid movement, giving her no opportunity to grab the phone or run into another room. Each man held one of her arms.

"Let go of me *now!*"

Dum made an inarticulate sound toward Dee. Simultaneously they released her. Dee, obviously the only one capable of actual speech, mumbled, "We aren't asking."

"So, what are you gonna do? Kidnap me?"

"No one will hurt you," Dee said. Dum croaked agreement. "But you must come. Mr. Hastings insists."

Maggie glared at the two men. "Mr. Hastings insists, does he? All right."

She scrawled a quick note to tack on the front door for her nephew, scooped up a full shopping bag, then preceded Dee and Dum out the door. She'd see Brendan Hastings, all right, but on her terms.

"By all means, gentlemen. Let's not keep your boss waiting."

Three

J.D. scanned the block, trying to find a parking place, anticipating Magnolia's shock when she opened the door and found him there instead of her "tall, blond and handsome" nephew. But would the shock result in her being irritated or pleased? Her unpredictability always kept him off guard—it was one of the things he enjoyed most about his relationship with her.

When Jasmine had called a couple of weeks ago to invite him to join them for New Year's Eve, he'd turned her down, not wanting to encourage Magnolia by being there. Then this morning he'd gotten word that Hastings was back in town, and J.D. had reinvited himself to the party.

He almost rear-ended the limousine double-parked—*Dios,* double-parked in front of Magnolia's apartment. He watched in horrified fascination as she came down the stairs, a bulky man on each side of her. Tall, blond and handsome was Hastings, not Matthew?

She didn't look his way but got into the limo calmly. She was going willingly? What the hell?

He muttered every curse he knew, English and Spanish. Blindly, he reached under his car seat and pulled out a custom computer the size of a cigar box. He flipped a switch, punched a few keys; a comforting beep greeted him. While stopped at a red light, he glanced at the digital numbers in the amber-lit screen.

Dios. She wasn't wearing the necklace.

He reached for his cell phone, searched his memory for a number and dialed, wishing he had the luxury of using a pay phone, where his call couldn't be easily intercepted and overheard.

"Yes?"

The soft, smoky voice wrapped him with a measure of relief.

"Do you know who this is?" he asked, keeping the limo in sight.

A tiny hesitation followed, then, "Why sure, lover. What can I do for you?"

"I need a favor."

The limousine turned into an underground parking garage, and Maggie was hustled into an elevator accessed only by a special key. She wondered if one would be needed to leave, as well.

Dum pushed the button marked *P*. In only a few seconds, the doors opened again and they faced a huge living room with an opulent view of San Francisco Bay. Brendan, dressed in a crisply pressed tuxedo, stood near the plate-glass window, a phone to his ear.

"Deal with it," he said, then turned and saw her. His voice changed from authoritative to mild as he smiled at her. "Quick and painless, though. It was a minor infraction, after all." His smile widened as he hung up the phone and walked toward her.

"Miss Walters. How very nice of you to join me."

"Stuff it, *Mr.* Hastings. 'Nice' has nothing to do with it. I was kidnapped."

Maggie watched Brendan fire a look of shocked inquiry to the two men who loomed behind her, blocking any attempt at escape. Then his mouth curved in a solicitous smile.

"I'm afraid my employees lack the finesse you're accustomed to, Miss Walters, but they mean no harm," he said, extending a hand in greeting.

She ignored the gesture. "They forced me to come here when I told them I had other plans. They gave me no choice. None. That's kidnapping."

Brendan cocked his head toward Dee and Dum, signaling they should depart. "You had other plans?" he repeated, taking her elbow and guiding her into the room with the glorious view. The silkiness of his voice didn't hide the intensity of the question.

"In fact, Mr. Hastings, I'd just turned down someone else's request for a date because of those plans. Just who do you think you are?"

"A man who's more than a little interested in you. May I fix you a drink? Some wine, perhaps?" He moved behind the bar.

Maggie took several calming breaths, knowing she had to be rational and reasonable.

Not waiting for her answer, he handed her a full glass. "Tell me about your plans. Were they with your sister, Jasmine?" Anticipating her next question, he said, "I made it my business to learn about you." He looked at her over the rim of his glass as he sipped his wine. "Try it, please. It's a delightful California zinfandel I just discovered."

She tasted the drink and murmured something complimentary.

He smiled. "Shall we sit?"

"I'll stand, thank you."

"As you wish." He stood an unintimidating two feet away and swirled the ruby rich liquid in his glass. "How was your Christmas?"

She set the bag she still carried at his feet. "I'm returning all your gifts. As I told you, I'm involved with someone."

"Not according to what I've heard."

"We've been discreet."

"Why? Is he married?"

"Of course not."

He smiled slightly. "My dear Miss Walters. You're not being honest with me."

"I'm not playing games."

"Ah, but you are."

She flinched as he touched her hair.

"You made it clear that you like the chase. So do I. But we're ready for the next step."

"I'm on my period." There. Factual and off-putting. She lifted her chin.

His eyes danced as he inched closer. "I'm not so crude as to expect you to fall into bed with me. Alas, the next step I was suggesting was a night on the town. Dinner, dancing, a kiss to welcome the new year."

"And if I say no?"

"You wouldn't leave me to celebrate the new year alone, would you?"

"Mr. Hastings, I have other plans. Regardless, I have no interest."

His smile disintegrated. He plucked her still-full wineglass from her and returned to the bar, where he plunked down both glasses. "Then I must regretfully insist. I had hoped to do this properly, Miss Walters. I had hoped to share a lovely evening. But if you insist on casting me as the bully, I assure you, I can fill that role."

His tone of voice filled in every blank—he would get what he wanted, when he wanted it.

Icy calculation lingered in his eyes, a darkness distinctly at odds with his civilized demeanor. A shiver raced through her, distributing tentacles of fear and anger. She was in way over her head. She could either go along with him or fight him. *Some choice.*

"I don't care for orders," she said, the barest hint of concession in her voice.

He relaxed fractionally. "And I am accustomed to giving them, and having them obeyed without question. I apologize for treating you like staff instead of the beautiful woman I desire."

"If I don't call my sister, she'll have the entire San Francisco Police Department out looking for me. She raised me. She's very protective."

"And very pregnant. I'll get a message to her. Now, shall we go?"

The amount of information he had on her astounded her. "Where?"

He cupped her elbow and guided her toward the elevator. Dee and Dum appeared from nowhere. "The top floor of the Empress Hotel. I believe it's a setting worthy of showing off the lovely jewel that you are."

A public place meant safety. What could he do? Okay. She could manage this, manage *him*. Now she only had to figure out a way to avoid the midnight kiss he wanted. She'd start by ordering every item on the menu with garlic in it.

Maggie looked out a floor-to-ceiling window at the twinkling lights of San Francisco. The elegant restaurant where Brendan had brought her took up the entire twentieth floor of the Empress Hotel. The room was filled with revelers waiting to celebrate the new year.

"Maggie?"

Reluctantly, she faced Brendan, who was losing patience with her lack of interest. He leaned toward her.

"You would have permanent use of the penthouse, unlimited credit—whatever your heart desires."

As he listed the perks of the job he was offering, Maggie glanced around the restaurant, wondering what the servers made in tips. She made more than a decent income at the Carola, thanks to great tips, but the food here was even more expensive.

"I don't usually make an offer so freely," he continued, "but I know it would be good between us. Phenomenal, in fact."

Meaning you usually sample the wares first. Was she supposed to feel flattered because he didn't ask for a "test drive"?

She looked at the Caesar salad she hadn't yet taken a bite of, rolled a few croutons over some romaine leaves, then set her fork aside. She had to come up with some kind of answer. Something to placate him, yet not commit her to anything. She lifted her wineglass, stalling, mentally forming a sentence, then noticed patrons around them turning in their chairs, watching a woman glide through the restaurant, greeting people, her beaded, ankle-length, cardinal red gown capturing and holding everyone's gazes. She stopped at Brendan and Maggie's table.

"Why, hon, what a surprise to see you here!"

Maggie smiled as Misty Champion touched her shoulder, and she relaxed for the first time that evening. "Misty, hi."

"Brendan, happy new year."

He stood to shake Misty's hand. They exchanged pleasantries for a minute as Maggie wondered why he hadn't invited Misty tonight instead. She seemed much more suited to him.

"I'm headed to the little girls' room," Misty said to Maggie. "Keep me company?"

Maggie grabbed her purse and tossed her napkin on the table as she shot out of the seat, not giving Brendan a second to stop her. She linked her arm through Misty's and hustled her away. The bathroom door had barely closed behind them when Maggie grabbed her.

"I have a big favor to ask."

"Shoot."

"Could you help me get out of here? It's a long story, too long to explain right now, and Brendan isn't going to be happy, but I'm willing to risk sneaking out, even though I'm concerned about what he'll do."

"And well you should be, hon. In the river of life, he's a crocodile and you're a tadpole." She picked up a book of

Empress Hotel matches from the vanity counter, then pulled a cellular phone from her purse, and dialed. She oozed charm. "Hi, there, Jacques. This is Misty Champion...."

Maggie listened as Misty made the necessary arrangements to get her out of the sky-high restaurant, then Misty folded the phone and slid it back into her purse.

"Okay, it's all set, hon. Jacques will be right outside the door."

"Thanks, Misty. I owe you."

"Just tell me you've learned a lesson—don't bite off more man than you can chew."

"I didn't bite this one." She eyed the rest-room door. "I felt as close to helpless as I ever want to feel in my life. I was doing the best I could to handle him. But he's...a force unto his own. I'm afraid this is just the beginning of my problems with him. He's going to be furious that I dumped him."

"I'm afraid you're right, hon. Trust me, this is not a man you want to be involved with."

Maggie frowned. "Then I can't leave you with him. I got myself into this mess. I'll get myself out."

She patted Maggie's arm. "In another life, I dealt with men like him. I know what to do."

"No, I—"

"Just follow me out."

Maggie expected to see either Brendan, Tweedledee or Tweedledum looming outside the door. She saw only the maître d', Jacques, who whisked her through the kitchen. He indicated a door.

"You will find a service elevator on the other side," he said precisely.

"Thank you."

He nodded and retreated. Maggie pushed open the door and stepped through.

"Well, Alice, have you had enough adventures in wonderland?"

She whirled around. "Diego! How did you— What are you doing here?"

He strode toward her. "That's some dress you're almost wearing."

"Don't start," she warned, relief warring with anger at herself. "I'm not in the mood."

She marched to the elevator and punched the down button. Several times she looked over her shoulder. She jabbed the down button twice more. "Come on. Come on."

"Where's your coat?" Diego asked, coming up beside her.

"In the coat check, at the restaurant." She fired a glance his way. "This can't be a coincidence, your being here. Were you following me?"

"I'll tell you later."

Maggie shivered, not only from the cold but from residual fear. After a moment she felt his suit jacket being draped around her, warm and scented with the essence of him. "Thank you," she said tightly, embarrassed that he'd seen her vulnerable. And inordinately glad that he was there.

J.D. cupped her shoulders a moment, indulging himself. They shared a silent ride down the elevator and an equally silent walk to his car, leaving each other to their thoughts. He observed her rigid posture, felt the stiffness of his own muscles.

Damn it, he'd known she'd get in the way. More than that, she'd almost blown it for him, almost ruined the relationship he was building with Hastings by forcing J.D. to confront him. Worse yet, she'd almost gotten herself into a position he couldn't have extricated her from so easily. Thank God for Misty, who'd been able to keep him out of any public scene with Hastings.

Still silent, J.D. and Maggie navigated the hills of the city until they reached her apartment. They climbed the stairs in unison. He took the key from her and opened the door. She flicked on the living room light as she passed him.

"*Dios.*" He ran his hand down the long crack in her front door. "What happened here?"

She tugged his jacket closer. "One of Brendan's henchmen wouldn't take no for an answer."

He inspected the splintered wood, giving himself time to calm. He should have been there. He'd known Hastings was back. He knew the man wouldn't give up—his track record verified that.

J.D. shoved the door to close it.

He should have known she'd need him.

"I don't believe Hastings would have harmed you," he told her. *Not yet,* he thought, aware that Hastings liked to present a civilized facade for the world. J.D. leashed his temper, knowing anger would counter his purposes. "Control you, yes. But not harm."

"Oh? And controlling someone isn't harmful?"

"It isn't life threatening." He cupped her elbow and moved her to the couch. They sat several feet apart.

"I guess it depends on who's being controlled. And I wasn't in fear for my life, just my right to choose who I date. He's creepy."

"Creepy. Could you be more specific?"

"Just creepy. I don't know how to define it. It's a feeling, that's all. Why were you there, anyway?"

"I was invited to your sister's party. I was going to surprise you, pick up you and Matthew and take you there. When I arrived, I saw you getting into the limo. That didn't make sense to me so I followed."

"Was Misty there because of you?"

"She fit the scene. I didn't."

"He made me feel dirty," she said, burrowing farther into his suit jacket, then scowling. "I'd just finished making that new winter coat, too. The jerk. He'd better give it back to me." She stood. "I need to wash off my makeup and get out of this dress. You won't leave, will you?"

"No. Take time to have a shower if that would make you feel better."

When J.D. heard water running, he stood and wandered around the room, more than a little surprised at the disorder he found. A large wooden hoop held what appeared to be a block of quilting; a sewing machine and cabinet took up a substantial amount of space in one corner; a dressmaker's form was layered with a diaphanous white silky nightgown draped over a mold reminiscent of Magnolia's shapely body. He traced the lines with his eyes, appreciating the perfection of proportion he'd always been drawn to. His willpower had been stretched to the limit these many months of working beside her, watching her move with unintentional—and sometimes completely intentional—seductiveness. She'd flirted relent-lessly with him, feeling safe perhaps, or maybe just testing him. He'd rarely reacted openly. It was all he could offer her—self-control, protection and respect.

He had a job to do, and the job came first. Unfortunately, she had become part of his job.

He forced his gaze from the dress form, shifting instead to the opposite corner where a desk held a computer and printer. Stacks of papers were piled neatly beside it. He resisted the temptation to thumb through them.

After a few minutes, the bedroom door opened. She was bundled in a fluffy pink bathrobe over a long, flannel night-gown dotted with tiny flowers. Her hair hung straight and wet to her shoulders. Her cosmetic-free face glowed from the scrubbing she'd given it. He wished he had the right to hold her.

"I'm sorry for the clutter," she said, stuffing her hands in her pockets. "I'm redecorating the second bedroom, so every-thing's out here until I'm done."

"It's a nice home, Magnolia. I don't think I told you that last time. Very warm and inviting."

"I like it." She sat on the sofa and rested her feet on the coffee table.

"I didn't know you sewed."

"My second love. Major in English, minor in fashion. Yes, I know. It's an odd combination. But I have plans for both."

"Where's the necklace I gave you?"

Startled by the question that seemed to come from nowhere, she straightened a little. Her fingers feathered her throat. "It didn't go with what I wore tonight."

"I asked you not to take it off."

"But...I was wearing rhinestone earrings. The necklace is gold."

"Ah, I see. Fashion comes before sentiment."

"But—"

He waved a hand. "Never mind. Tell me what happened," he said, his tone softening as he sat beside her.

The phone rang.

He moved like a man possessed, curving his hand over the receiver before she could touch it. "If it's Hastings, let me listen, too," he said.

"Why?"

"Humor me, Magnolia." He passed her the receiver.

"Hello?"

"Well, my little fox, you led this hound on a merry chase."

Maggie tipped the phone Diego's way at the first sound of Brendan's voice. "I decided I needed to be with my family, after all."

"Yet you're at home, not at your sister's house."

"My head hurt. I wouldn't have been good company."

The ensuing silence made the lie seem bigger. She squirmed a little.

"I'll forgive you, Miss Walters, this time. I underestimated how much you resented my arranging the evening. Next time I'll ask. But mark my words, I will have you—one way or another. Good night."

Diego took the phone and pressed the disconnect button "You handled that very well."

Maggie expelled a sound of disgust. "Can you believe him?" The pitch of her voice broadcast her building fury. She pushed herself off the sofa. "'I will have you.' Ha! In his dreams."

"Magnolia—"

"'One way or another.' What does that mean? Willing or not?"

"Calm down."

"Dead or—" She stopped short and pressed a hand to her

mouth, her mind filled with the memory of Brendan on the telephone in his penthouse. Quick and *painless,* he'd said. Quick and painless?

She sought Diego then, watched him walk to her, felt his hands curve around her arms as if to steady her. "Dead or alive?" she whispered.

"Take it easy. You're safe."

"I thought he was just another dictatorial, powerful man, used to getting his own way." She sorted it out in her head. "He's more than that, isn't he? That's why you're so worried. He's some kind of criminal."

"That's the rumor."

J.D. tightened his hold on her as she pulled back in dawning awareness. He couldn't give her details. She wore her feelings on her face, and he couldn't take the chance she'd slip up. But two young women had been murdered, and the evidence pointed to Hastings. Magnolia could not be the third. He'd see to that.

"How do you know so much about him?" she asked.

He saw suspicion cloud her eyes. *Be careful,* he warned himself. *She's way too perceptive.*

"You chatter with customers. I listen."

"Are you sure about him?" Her gaze wandered over his face. "Of course you're sure. And Misty said— She called him a crocodile. But I don't understand. He's a member of the Carola. The people there—"

"Have to be rich, powerful or famous. That's all."

She pulled away to perch on the edge of the couch. "So, I've shattered the ego of a powerful man. What does he do about it? Does he get me fired?"

J.D. sat across from her. "If so, he'd be advertising his failure to win you over."

"Pride. Okay, that's good. But he's undoubtedly ticked off."

"Extremely."

"You're a big help."

He found he could actually smile. "Maybe it's time to visit your mother," he suggested.

Her mouth dropped open. "In New Orleans? You're kidding. That'd be worse than anything Brendan had in mind."

He said her name softly. She was losing her fear. He needed her to understand that Hastings posed a real danger. "I really think you should go."

"Go into hiding, you mean." She shook her head. "He'd find me at my mother's in an instant. He already seems to know everything there is to know about me. I'm not running. I'm not hiding. I have a life to live. A job. School. A niece or nephew on the way. Responsibilities. I can handle this."

"No, Magnolia. You can't. Not alone."

"Yes, I can."

He leaned forward. "Don't underestimate him. He's a genuine power and a genuine threat."

"He's harassing me. I can call the police. I could get a restraining order or something. Patrick would help me."

"Your brother-in-law's attention should be focused only on your sister and the baby right now. You can't ask him to get involved." He settled back in the chair again. His gaze held hers. "Looks like you're stuck with me."

"Stuck?"

"There's only one solution that I can see."

"What's that?"

"You're going to have to marry me."

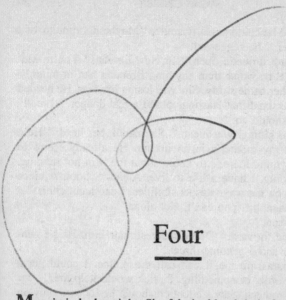

Four

Maggie jerked upright. She felt the blood drain from her face as her mouth moved uselessly to form some sort of reply.

"We won't share a bed," he assured her. "The marriage can be annulled when it's safe to do so. Until then, you would have my protection."

"Protection," she repeated, fitting the word into her situation. His protection, but at what cost?

"Hastings follows his own code of ethics. He won't touch another man's wife, another man's leavings, although he'll cheat on his wife without a second thought."

"He's married?"

"With three children."

"How—" she stopped momentarily, trying to make sense of it all "—how do you know all this?"

"It's my job to know about him—about everyone who comes to the Carola. You're going to have to trust me, Magnolia. I won't let any harm come to you, that I promise."

"I need facts, Diego. Concrete facts to support so drastic a solution."

He leaned forward. "Fact. Hastings threatened you. Fact. No one can stop him from coming to your place of employment—unless he does something drastic enough to get himself kicked out. By then it may be too late.

"Fact. Rumors are not proof. The police won't get involved based on rumors. Fact. We don't know exactly how far this man would go, particularly when, as you say, his ego has been shattered."

He sat back, seeming to relax. "I say an ounce of prevention is worth *more* than a pound of cure. I have offered you a way out. If we marry, not only should it halt his pursuit of you, it puts us in physical proximity for me to protect you, in case…well, just in case. Put your stubbornness aside and think this through."

Maggie closed her eyes and pressed her fingers to her temples, which had started to throb. "I need some aspirin," she said. "I'll be right back."

She escaped into the bathroom, shutting him out with a deliberate click of the lock. She dumped two tablets into her hand, washed them down with a full glass of water. Then she looked into the mirror, not liking what she saw there—the fragility that lingered. She was tempted to give in to it. Tempted to let Diego handle everything, to take care of her.

Tempted. But not giving in.

She couldn't remember a time in her life when she hadn't dreamed of meeting a wonderful man, falling hopelessly in love, walking down the aisle to him in a gown she'd designed and made, and pledging to love, honor and cherish him forever.

Her dream hadn't come from any shining example—her mother had been married six times—but Maggie still believed in one man, one love, one marriage for a lifetime.

Part of that dream involved a glorious marriage proposal in which her husband-to-be declared his undying love and devotion.

Never once had she imagined, "You're going to have to marry me."

Well, so much for romance, she thought, relegating her dreams to a shadowed corner of her heart. Fantasy had no place in the reality of the moment, the reality of her situation.

She filled the water cup again, drank deeply, stalling.

Why wasn't he confiding in her? He wanted her to trust him but he didn't trust *her.* How could they have even a temporary relationship without trust?

Temporary. She stared at the sink. The truth was that Brendan or not, trust or not, *love* or not, she wanted to marry Diego. The feelings that had simmered in her for so long had to have names attached to them, had to find their place. He'd kept her at arm's length, never giving them a chance to see what could happen.

She could use this time to create a home with him. They would share the same space, eat together, have time for conversation. She couldn't tell him why she was saying yes, of course. He needed his own fantasy of protecting her. And *maybe* she was a little worried about Brendan, as well.

But that didn't mean she couldn't handle it.

She ran a brush through her hair, noting the color was back in her face. Good. She didn't want him to remember her weakness but her strength.

J.D. turned when the door opened. He'd been staring blindly at her apartment, imagining himself living with her. When that vision became overwhelming, he'd moved to the window to watch the street, which was better than examining why he'd offered her marriage. He could have forced her to a safe house. Why hadn't he? Fact. He didn't want her out of his sight.

He saw refusal in the way she carried herself, in the color in her cheeks and the fire in her eyes. He was set to argue again.

"I'll change," she said. "We can head to Lake Tahoe and get married tonight."

"No." A lifetime of controlling his emotions allowed him to meet her halfway across the room. He would not show his relief, which threatened to break him in two. "We'll do this right. We'll have a real wedding, with newspaper announcements, invitations, everything. No, not the newspaper, I think. But Hastings has to believe this is genuine, Magnolia. You can't tell anyone differently."

Her tone was just as businesslike. "If you want Jasmine to believe it, I have to make my dress, and that's going to take some time. There's no way she'd accept that I'd get married without making my dream gown."

"How much time do you need?"

Maggie moved to pick up a calendar. "January twenty-first. That gives us three weeks. I'll have a week of semester break left, so we could pretend to honeymoon then. I want Jasmine to stand up with me, and her baby's due in six weeks. I think if we add all those facts together, it's a believable scenario for a hurried wedding."

"I'll pay for the dress and—"

She interrupted. "Oh, no, you won't. You want this traditional, right? I pay for the gown. That's traditional."

"There is a rule about that? Where is it written?"

Machismo oozed through his control. Perversely, she encouraged it, needing some kind of emotion from him. "In every bride magazine published. Don't you know anything?"

"Why would I know that?" His voice gathered volume. "I have not been married before."

"Then you'll have to acknowledge me as the expert. And I say I pay for my own gown. I have enough money saved."

"But—"

"But nothing, Mr. Macho. You're doing *me* the favor, here. You're protecting *me*. The least I can do is pay for it."

"Magnolia, if you make the dress of your dreams for this wedding, what will you do when you really marry?"

Tears welled. Couldn't he let her have her fantasy for just a minute? Turning away, she set down the calendar. "I'm too tired to think about this anymore. Why don't you go home and we'll talk in the morning."

"Like hell."

He'd come up behind her with the stealth of a panther. He cupped her shoulders, turning her to face him. He lifted her chin and examined her face. She stared right back at him, hating the tears that threatened to spill, hating that he saw.

"You think I would leave you here alone?" he asked softly, gruffly. "I told you I would protect you. Tomorrow I'll replace your door and install a security system. But tonight you will sleep, knowing I'm here, knowing you're safe. Do you have any objections to that?"

She shook her head, relieved and uncomfortable at the same time. One pressure removed and one gained. Would it be like this forever?

"There's a sleeper-sofa in the spare bedroom," she said. "I'll get bedding for you."

"I'll use the couch here. A pillow and a blanket will do."

She gathered bedding from the linen closet and made up the sofa for him, aware of him standing still and silent behind her, watching her fuss. Straightening, she turned around. "Thank you for everything."

He nodded. "Good night."

J.D. watched her hurry into the bedroom and shut the door. He let out a breath and stood hunched over, his breathing erratic, still fighting his need to take her in his arms, her tears a siren call of feminine need for masculine comfort.

He ran his hands through his hair as he moved into the bathroom to wash up, needing a shower, but not daring to have his hearing limited by the running water.

He turned out the living room light and undressed to his slacks. Pulling his pistol from his ankle holster, he laid it on the coffee table, a habitual, if probably unnecessary, precaution. He moved to the living room window and rested a bare foot on the low ledge of the window as he observed the street below.

Time passed, exactly how much, he wasn't sure, but long enough for her to have fallen asleep. He found himself at her bedroom door, his hand on the knob. Magically, it turned and he moved through the shadowy, moonlit room to where he could just see her dark hair fanned against the light fabric of her pillow. He crouched beside the bed, enjoying the distinctive, delicate scent that permeated the room before he realized she was watching him.

The bedclothes rustled as she raised up on an elbow. She rested a hand on his chest a tentative moment before she stroked him, conforming her palm to the contours of his muscles, across, down, and up, with careful caresses, her gaze never leaving his. Her fingertip brushed one nipple, stayed to tease as it tightened, then treated the other to equal pleasure. She followed an imaginary line from his throat to his navel and back up, lightly disturbing the sparse hair dusting his chest. He didn't move a muscle. His body betrayed him, anyway, as need pooled deep inside him.

"Who are you?" she asked.

His stomach lurched. "I don't know what you're asking."

"I've been lying here thinking about you. You're so strong. Stronger than I even imagined," she said, her voice hushed. "You hide that strength from the world. Why?"

"I am what you see."

"No."

"Yes, Magnolia. Do not make me some fantasy hero, some mystery man. I am no more than I seem."

"You're complicated. You have a strong body, even stronger principles. You're intelligent. Yet you seem content with the work you do. Don't frown at me. It was not a criticism, but an observation." She paused. "Do you have goals, Diego? Dreams? Are you content being a maître d'? I think you could do anything you set your mind to."

She toyed with the hair below his navel, her nails lightly scraping his skin. *Madre de Dios.* Taking a deep breath, he curved his hand over hers, tucking her fingers within his. "I'm doing what I must. But make no mistake. This marriage will be in name only. Do not try to change that. You will only get hurt."

She pulled free as if to retreat. Instead, she pressed two fingers to the placket of his slacks.

"What are you going to do about that?" she asked in a near whisper. With agonizing slowness, she traced the hard length.

"Control it." He lifted her hand away more carefully than she deserved for teasing him. "Go to sleep."

"You want me."

"And that pleases you, doesn't it?" He brought his face close to hers. "It means nothing, Magnolia. What is significant is what I do about it."

"What if I continue to try?"

"I would hope you have enough respect for me not to make a difficult situation impossible. Even I have limits to my control. But I need to awaken each morning with a clear conscience. I'm counting on you not to push."

"I don't think I'll ever understand you."

He stood. "That's probably for the best."

J.D. closed the bedroom door behind him, then walked with measured strides to the sofa. Sinking onto it, he rested his head in his hands until his need for her faded. He pulled up the quilt and stretched out the length of the couch, closing his eyes. He'd always wondered how aggressive she'd be. Now he knew. She was all smoke and fire, as he'd always suspected. And he wanted her more than ever.

Maggie gave her sister credit. Jasmine waited until the last Rose Parade float disappeared from the television screen before reacting to the news Maggie and Diego had dropped on her hours earlier. The sisters were alone in Jasmine's living room, Diego off taking care of Maggie's broken door, Jasmine's husband, Patrick, attempting to make breakfast, along with her teenage children, Matthew and Raine.

The boisterous conversation from the kitchen wrapped the house in a cocoon of family warmth, and Maggie wallowed in the atmosphere she'd longed to create for herself and a family of her own. She watched and waited as Jasmine, settled comfortably in a recliner, braided the fringe on the afghan Patrick had insisted she keep over her lap. Her white-blond hair and soft gray eyes gave an impression of coolness. Maggie knew better.

Maggie smiled as her sister drew a breath, held it a few seconds, then let it all out. She combed the braid free with her fingers, obviously stalling.

"Come on, Jazz, say what's on your mind."

"How could you keep this from me? I didn't even know you and J.D. were dating, and here you are, engaged. Why didn't you say anything?"

"Everything happened pretty fast."

"But a wedding in three weeks? Why the hurry? And how can we manage it?"

"We don't, Jazz. I do. The last thing you need is a wedding to handle at this stage of your pregnancy."

"Maggie! Are you pregnant?"

Maggie laughed.

"I take it that means no. All right, then, at least let us hire a wedding consultant to take care of the details. You can't do it all. There's so much to consider."

"All right," Maggie said, deciding she could repay her sister later. "It does seem a little overwhelming, especially on top of making my gown. But the wedding itself is going to be small."

"Are you bringing Mom up for it?"

Ignoring the fist that seemed to have slammed into her stomach, Maggie stood and moved around the room, stopping at the fireplace to look at a photograph of their mother on the mantel. "I suppose I'll have to invite her. I don't imagine she'll come, especially not if she has to bring her newest husband along. I'm sure she's lied about her age again. She'd be too embarrassed to let him see she has daughters who are forty-one and thirty."

"I know you resent her, Maggie, but she's still your mother. You need to stop letting the past matter so much."

"She never wanted me, Jazz. She was forty-four years old when I was born. I just got in the way."

"She could have had an abortion, but she didn't. And I think you turned out all right."

"Thanks to you. If you hadn't been there, I don't know what would have happened to me." Maggie knelt beside her sister's chair. She envied Jasmine her family, even if she didn't envy her pregnancy at forty-one. "You know how it was with Mom, Jazz. She was like my grandmother but she kept trying to be like a sister."

"I know. Oh! Feel this." Jasmine pulled Maggie's hand to press against where the baby kicked.

They shared the moment, then Jasmine said quietly, "You know I think the world of J.D. But I'm not seeing between you and him what I should be seeing."

"What's that?"

"You didn't touch each other, Maggie. You should be having a hard time keeping your hands off each other. You should be making everyone sick watching you. You should be dying to get home and make love, not spending the day with your pregnant sister and her family."

Maggie propped her elbows on the arm of Jasmine's chair, then rested her chin in her hands. "We haven't made love. We're not going to before the wedding."

Jasmine stared. "Oh my God, you're serious. Why?"

"Diego wants it that way. I'm going to respect his wishes."

Jasmine started to laugh, then couldn't stop. She laughed so long and so hard, her husband and children poked their heads out of the kitchen to see what was going on. Maggie shushed her sister, making her promise not to tell, announcing to the others that they could go back into the kitchen.

"I have to tell Patrick," Jasmine whispered, still clutching her belly. "I can't keep secrets from him."

"Yes, you can."

Her eyes sparkled. "Not this one. Oh, this is priceless, Maggie. You've been so hot for him for so long and he's going to make you wait. I can't believe it. You know, I just remembered what he said about you once. We were talking about that woman he was dating for a while, Adrianna—"

Maggie muttered an uncomplimentary remark.

"You were so jealous of her. J.D. told me she was not the kind of woman a man marries. He would only marry a woman pure of heart."

"Chauvinist." Maggie said the word automatically, but her mind wandered with curiosity. She sat back on her heels and considered a thought. Maybe he had suggested a marriage of convenience because he wanted her to stay pure—whatever that meant to him—for her "real" husband. She'd have to ask him.

"I need to talk to you about something," Maggie said after Diego explained her new security system he'd installed earlier in the day, including the panic buttons he'd placed in various locations around the apartment. "Can we sit down for a few minutes?"

He waited until she sat on the sofa before taking a chair across from her.

"Coward," she said lightly.

"You wanted something, Magnolia?"

"Jasmine knows something isn't quite right between us."

"In what way?"

"She says we don't act like an engaged couple. According to her, we should be all kissy-faced and honey-bunnied."

"Kissy-faced and...what? I suppose that means we weren't demonstrative enough to suit her."

"You've never heard of kissy-faced? I made up honey-bunnied." She waved a dismissive hand. "I told her we weren't going to sleep together before the wedding. She thought it was hysterically funny."

"So that explains the looks she kept giving me over dinner and the comment she whispered as she hugged me goodbye."

"What'd she say?"

"That she and Patrick had a bet on the outcome of the next three weeks."

"I asked her not to tell Patrick."

J.D. watched her tap her foot rhythmically against the floor. "I suppose now you expect me to be publicly affectionate."

"You're the one who wanted everything to look real."

He couldn't quite decipher her tone of voice—slightly hostile, more than a little defensive. "All right. I can do that."

"Well, don't overdo it. She'd get suspicious of that, too." Her foot continued to bounce.

"Was there something else, Magnolia?"

"Do you have it in your head that I'm a virgin?"

Five

The words shocked him speechless, coming out of nowhere as they did.

"Because I'm not."

"I didn't expect you were," he said tightly. He stood and swept up his jacket before heading to the door.

She followed. "Although I might as well be." She had the satisfaction of seeing his stride hitch a little.

"Meaning?" The word was tossed out reluctantly.

"Meaning the few experiences I had were duds."

"I don't want to talk about this."

"Well, I do. Is that why you won't sleep with me? Because you think I'm saving myself for my 'true' husband?"

He kept walking. She dogged his steps.

"It doesn't matter, Magnolia."

"Then why can't we sleep together? We can be adult about it."

"Like hell. If we sleep together, we can't get an annulment."

"No one would know but us. Diego, I don't think we can live together and not make love, not without killing each other."

"I can. And I won't lie to the court, either."

"'You're a better man than I am, Gunga Din.'"

"What the hell is that supposed to mean?"

"It was a quote. Rudyard Kipling."

"I know who said it. I can't figure out why you—" He stopped. She was doing it again, goading him into a reaction. He turned around when he reached the door. "Just what is your problem?"

"I don't know," she answered, her eyes full of bewilderment. "Damn," she said, turning from him. "Damn. Damn. Damn."

"Aw, hell, Magnolia." He laid his hands on her shoulders and pulled her to him. "Come here."

He enfolded her in his embrace, tightening his hold until their bodies touched all the way down. Ah, but she felt good in his arms. Too good. A tiny crack split his control. He rested his cheek against her hair, felt her fingers dig into his back, and he cherished the moment so long denied him. *"Novia,"* he said soothingly. "It's all right. We'll work everything out."

"I don't mean to be so difficult," she said, finally relaxing against him. Her arms settled loosely at his waist. She rubbed her cheek against his shoulder. "It's just that twenty-four hours ago, my life was simple. I knew what to expect every day. I knew what my future would be. Everything's been turned upside down and I'm having a hard time adjusting."

"Why don't you let me do the worrying, and you just try to relax."

"How can I relax when I have buttons I can push that will connect me with the police department if someone breaks in?"

"I know it's a lot to ask. But think about this. If I expected that Hastings would do something, you couldn't get me out of here with a court order. But I'm going home. I'm being overly cautious, that's all."

Maggie pushed away from him. "I don't understand why

you're willing to help me like this. What do *you* get out of it?"

"A good-deed badge to sew on my sash? What does it matter?" He opened the door. "I forgot to tell you that your new winter coat is hanging in your closet."

"It is? Did Brendan send it over?"

"I got it back."

"From the restaurant?"

"From Hastings."

He shut the door behind him, leaving her with even more questions. Definitely a man of mystery. And definitely much more than he seemed.

She yanked open the door and yelled down the stairs. "What does *novia* mean?"

"Sweetheart," he called over his shoulder. "But don't take it too seriously. I called my favorite dog that, too."

From just outside the door to the Carola's dining room, J.D. heard Maggie humming within. He relaxed some as he moved to the maître d's podium. He'd called her ten times during the day, although he left messages only twice. She hadn't returned his calls.

At least she had been wearing the necklace.

"Hi."

He hadn't heard her come up beside him. She stood smiling tentatively at him, her bright blue eyes examining his face as she seemed to gauge his mood. It irritated the hell out of him. *She* was supposed to be the unpredictable one.

He lounged against the podium and crossed his arms. "How was your day?"

"Busy. Tiring. There's a lot to do. Jazz and I interviewed several wedding coordinators, then we bought the fabric for my gown."

"I'd like to be included in the planning."

Her eyes opened wide. "Would you? I hadn't realized."

"It's my wedding, too, Magnolia."

"Such as it is."

He put a finger to her lips, then bent close to her. Close enough to fill his head with her perfume. "The only place we can talk freely is in your apartment. Here, and everywhere else, we are a happily engaged couple."

"Are we going to announce it to everyone now?"

"We'd better. Hastings made a reservation for tonight and he already knows. I think our friends would be disappointed to hear it through him." He straightened again, holding her scent in his lungs, letting it filter through his body to tease him, as it was intended to do.

"How does Brendan know?"

"I told him when I got your coat back."

"What was his reaction?"

He'd laughed. J.D. couldn't tell her that—that Hastings didn't believe the engagement. But their business relationship required circumspection between the two men. J.D. would play his role.

"He wished us well," he said.

"Why don't I believe that?"

"Why didn't you return my calls today, Magnolia?"

Maggie mirrored his pose by leaning an elbow on the podium beside him and also crossing her arms, wishing she'd stop shivering every time he said her name in that soft, warm voice he used to tease information from her. "I would have gladly done so, if I had your phone number."

She had the pleasure of seeing his skin draw taut over his cheekbones before he slid a piece of paper from a drawer.

"Here is my home phone, pager, cellular phone and address."

"And to think I couldn't find you today," she murmured, awed by his accessibility. She tucked the paper in her pocket. "If you really want to be involved in the plans, we need to talk about a guest list for the wedding so that we can order invitations."

"Tonight, after work. I have a couple of things to discuss with you, as well."

"Okay. Then tomorrow you can come help me paint the second bedroom."

"As long as it isn't pink."

"Deal. I'm assuming we'll be living at my place."

"My apartment would be too small for the two of us. One bedroom."

Works for me, Maggie thought.

"I noticed that Judge Shaunnessey has a reservation tonight. What would you think of asking him to perform the wedding ceremony?" Diego asked.

"Can he still do that, since he's retired?"

"We can ask him."

"Okay. I think it's a wonderful idea. He's a sweetheart."

"A sweetheart."

Maggie grinned. She loved the way he repeated the things she said that baffled or intrigued him, not phrasing a question but simply repeating the words. "You didn't know him before his hair started graying. He had the brightest red hair you'd ever want to see, and we all thought he'd have a temper to match. But nothing ruffles him."

"An excellent quality in a judge."

She flattened a hand against his chest to smooth the pleats of his shirt. "Nothing seems to ruffle you, either."

His hand curved around hers. His eyes filled with warmth as he drew up her hand and pressed a kiss to her palm. "You'd be surprised, Magnolia."

She held her breath for a minute, then she frowned in understanding. "Who's watching us?"

"Joe and Ruthie."

The bartender and a fellow waitress. "What are they doing?"

He kissed her hand again. He didn't appear to be looking anywhere but at her. Maggie was impressed.

"Elbowing each other," he said. "Snickering. I think we'd better go make the announcement."

Maggie watched him show surprise at the presence of their

co-workers. She shook her head, hiding a smile. He was good. Damn good. She was glad to be along for the ride.

The evening was perfect. Their co-workers offered hand-shakes, hugs and deafening good wishes. Judge Shaunnessey agreed to perform the wedding ceremony. Brendan Hastings canceled his reservation. Then the evening got even better when Misty Champion came in alone as the club was closing.

"I was stuck at the warehouse today and yesterday," she said to Maggie as they stood in the lobby.

"You spent New Year's Day at the warehouse?"

"I've never been able to give up control of the business. No matter how many people I hire to take charge, I still follow up on things myself. My curse." She shrugged. "The spring line heads to stores in a couple of weeks. We've got stock to the rafters. It's going to be our best year ever. But I'm sure you're more interested in what happened with Brendan."

"Every detail. I've been really worried about you. I left a bunch of messages for you."

"That's why I'm here. Well, he didn't miss a beat, hon. In fact, he almost seemed to be expecting me instead of you."

"So he treated you all right?"

"He was edgy, but not rude. We spent an hour together, then we went our own ways."

"I'll never be able to thank you enough." Maggie turned as she heard Diego's voice and saw him walking with Judge Shaunnessey. Diego came to Maggie's side and put an arm around her.

"Did you tell her?" he asked.

"Not yet."

"You're getting married!" Misty exclaimed, looking from one to the other.

"On January twenty-first. It'll be a small wedding, but you're invited, of course," Maggie said as the women hugged.

Misty kissed J.D.'s cheek. "You must have the wedding at my house. And the reception. Please," Misty implored them.

"I have the perfect room. It will hold fifty people comfortably. Is that enough?"

"But, Misty—" Maggie began.

"Unless you have a church lined up, of course."

Not hardly, Maggie thought. Their marriage of convenience wasn't worthy of such a setting. "No. But still, we can't ask that of you. I interviewed wedding coordinators today—"

"I'll arrange everything. All you need to do is show up. Call me tomorrow and we'll get together. Oh! I'm so happy for you both. Two of my most favorite people in the world. I won't take no for an answer."

Maggie felt Diego squeeze her hand when she would have protested further. "All right. All right." She laughed. "No wonder you've succeeded so well in business. You just bulldoze your way into agreement. Misty, do you know Judge Shaunnessey? He's going to perform the ceremony."

"We know each other well," the judge said, sandwiching Misty's hand between both of his. "How have you been?"

She tugged lightly. "Very well, Duncan. And you?"

"Making do."

Maggie watched the tension sparking between them. The judge's voice was low, soft and relaxed. Yet his eyes held such intensity as he stared into Misty's, and his thumbs drew circles on her skin. And Misty—well, her face flushed even as she lifted her chin and withdrew her hand.

"Call me," she said to Maggie. She opened the front door, then looked back. "Good night, Duncan."

"Be well, Misty."

He cares about her, Maggie realized finally as she analyzed his expression, one of sadness and longing. "Judge Shaunnessey, thank you again for agreeing to marry us."

"It's my honor and privilege, my dear." He kissed Maggie's cheek and exchanged a handshake with Diego. "Thank you for asking me."

"He's in love with Misty," Maggie said to Diego after the judge left. "Why haven't I seen that before? I've noticed them staring at each other across the dining room."

"Let them work it out themselves, Magnolia."

"You knew? You really do watch and listen, don't you?"

They headed toward the locker rooms to change.

"From now on, I'd like to pick you up for work and take you home, if you don't mind."

"Nifty change of subject, Diego." She grinned. "Sure. I think that would be great. Ah. You had expected an argument from me. I'm so sorry to disappoint you."

"You never disappoint me, Magnolia. Surprise me, yes. But not disappoint. I'll meet you back here in a few minutes."

"So, that's it? You've got a pretty short list of guests," Maggie said, tossing the pad of paper onto the coffee table.

They sat a couple of feet apart on the sofa. Each held a glass of wine and had been nibbling on sourdough bread and cheddar cheese.

"You can pick up the balance. I don't care about an even amount."

"I don't have that many to add myself. My family. A few friends from school."

"No old boyfriends to invite?"

"I told you before that I haven't had a serious relationship."

"Correction. You told me they were duds in the lovemaking department. That's different."

She cocked her head. "So now you want to talk about it? You didn't last night."

"I have thought about it since then. If you need to talk about it, then I'm willing to listen."

He didn't miss the smile she tried to hide behind her wine-glass.

"Forget it." He set his own glass on the table and picked up the pad of paper. "What is left for us to decide?"

"The time of day, flowers, um, food, I suppose."

He threw down the pad. "What does it mean when you say they were duds? And quit looking so smug, Magnolia. I admit, you piqued my curiosity."

"What do you want to know? How many men? How many times? How big were—"

"Stop right there."

"—their hands?"

"Funny."

"Well, Diego, I don't know what kind of information you're looking for. According to books I've read and conversations I've overheard, I should have felt the earth move."

"You have never climaxed?"

If his bluntness startled her, she didn't show it. "Of course I have." She swallowed some wine. "Sort of." She pressed a finger to her lips as she added, "I think."

"If you have to think about it, you haven't."

She looked directly at him. "Unless you intend to do something about this conversation, I'd suggest you abandon the topic."

He wished he'd never brought up the subject. Did she think he could resist that kind of temptation? To bring her to climax when no other man had? *Madre de Dios.*

Desire pulled at him. All she had to do was look at him to discover the truth, just as he could see the truth in the twin points of her nipples beneath her T-shirt. She hadn't bothered with a bra, that had been evident from the moment she'd taken off her jacket when they arrived at her apartment. And he'd watched her breasts sway as she'd moved around her kitchen preparing their snack.

He acknowledged this moment as his last chance to back out—which would certainly please his boss. Callahan's shout could have been heard in Washington, D.C., as he'd threatened to pull J.D. off the assignment. But negotiations with Hastings had gone too far and too well to attempt a change now.

Except that J.D. no longer had only himself to look out for, but Magnolia as well.

He pushed himself off the couch and crossed the room. Plucking his jacket off the coatrack, he carried it with him when he returned to her.

"You're leaving? I thought you wanted to discuss the wedding," she said.

Last chance. The words rang in his head again, then faded. From inside his coat pocket he pulled out an object and passed it to her.

"What's this?" she asked, turning it over. "Oh, a pager. Is this yours?"

"It's yours. Jasmine and Patrick asked me to get it for you. You've been so worried about her not being able to get in touch with you when she goes into labor. She said to tell you just to leave it on all the time, then she'll only have to dial one number and be able to find you. Make sure you change the battery when it says so across the pager screen. Here are some extras for you."

"This is great." Maggie listened as he gave her instructions on using the pager, then she set it aside. She watched him dig in his coat pocket again but couldn't see whatever he withdrew, as he closed his fingers around it.

"I think you should be wearing a ring," he said, opening his hand. "This was my grandmother's."

A brilliant-cut diamond perched in the center, surrounded by deep blue sapphires shaped like daisy petals. "Oh, Diego." She looked into his eyes as they darkened to almost black. "I couldn't. I just couldn't."

"It suits you."

"But—"

"Humor me, Magnolia."

She closed her eyes briefly. "I'd be honored."

He reached for her left hand, then slid the ring on her finger, finding a perfect fit.

Maggie held out her hand to admire it. "Why is one sapphire attached to the band instead of the diamond in the middle?"

"'He loves me.'"

"I beg your pardon?"

"You know. The game people play with flower petals. 'He

loves me, he loves me not.' There are seven so it will always end up 'he loves me.'"

"Oh! That's sweet. Your grandfather was a romantic." She laughed self-consciously. "I wish you'd quit giving me such incredible pieces of jewelry when I'm not wearing anything worthy of the moment."

"You are a beautiful woman, Magnolia. You don't need clothes to make you more so." He smiled. "You know what I mean."

He stayed another hour as they discussed other wedding details, and watched her sneak glances at the ring again and again, reinforcing his decision to give it to her.

He'd had no intention of giving her his grandmother's ring. In fact, he'd already arranged to rent a rather ordinary one from a local jeweler when his father placed this one in his hands.

The delicate beauty of it seemed right. He probably should have stayed with his original decision but he was tired of trying to analyze and rationalize everything that had happened in the past few days.

They were getting married. That was that. The reasons mattered, but they couldn't be changed.

This was Magnolia, after all. The one woman he'd been attracted to beyond the physical. In fairness to her, he hadn't encouraged her, knowing he wasn't free to pursue any kind of relationship until this job was over, knowing she was a woman who would burrow into his life and stay, if given the opportunity.

He hadn't let himself think about the future. One of the reasons he'd been assigned this job was his lack of attachments. Now he had an Achilles' heel.

And Hastings knew it.

It was still critical that he believe their marriage. Although J.D. no longer feared Hastings using Magnolia for his own pleasure—and the pleasure of others when he tired of her—J.D. also knew that Hastings could and would still use her against him. She had to be guarded and protected, because if his cover was blown, she'd be the first one that Hastings went after. He couldn't let that happen.

When she smothered a yawn, he stood. "Let me help you clean up, then I'll leave."

They carried the remains of their snack into the kitchen. Maggie stopped at the sink and turned on the faucet as she set down the dishes. Diego came up behind her. He reached around her to rinse the glasses.

Coils of anticipation rooted Maggie into stillness.

"Tired?" he asked quietly, close to her ear.

"Um." Her mind went blank for a few seconds. "Um, yes. But I'm generally up this late. It's hard to go to sleep right away after work."

"What do you do?"

She drew a shaky breath as he turned off the faucet that she'd left running. Then he leaned a hip against the counter and met her gaze, their bodies almost touching.

"It depends," she said. "Sometimes I sew. Sometimes I do homework. Um, sometimes I write. Have I told you about the magazine articles— What are you doing?"

His gaze had dropped. He was staring at her breasts.

"You've been driving me crazy," he said.

She angled toward him, unconsciously pushing her shoulders back, feeling her nipples tighten under his unwavering inspection. "What did I do?"

"You're not wearing anything under that shirt. I've watched you all night. The soft sway of your breasts. Your nipples growing hard again and again, teasing me. You are more…well, just more than I would have guessed."

Maggie touched his cheek. She brushed a thumb across his lips. "Kiss me."

He shook his head.

"Don't you think we need to practice?"

"Perhaps you do, Magnolia. I, for one, have had plenty of practice."

She hated every woman he'd ever touched. Kissed. Pleasured. "I mean together. You and me. When the judge pronounces us husband and wife, we'll have to kiss. I don't even know whether you tip your head to the right or the left."

"I assure you, *novia,* we'll manage just fine."

"You are the most strong-willed man I've ever met."

"I'm just a man. Like any other man."

"Show me."

The delicate balance between real and pretend exhausted him. What he wanted was a far cry from what he could take.

"Just touch me for a minute," she said quietly into his silence. "Somewhere. Anywhere. Just for a minute. Please."

She came into his arms as if born to be there. He felt her shudder, heard her moan his name softly. Her arms tightened around him as she burrowed closer.

"You feel so good," she whispered. "So right."

He slid his hands under her T-shirt and she arched into him. He spread his hands across her back and she drew up on tiptoes. He dragged his thumbs down the sides of her breasts and she hissed.

Putting a little distance between them, he let the backs of his hands glide under the velvet heat of her breasts, their weight settling like twin comforters.

He needed to stop this now. Now...

He ran his fingertips over her nipples, pebbled into hard, tempting knots. This time her moan rang loud and uncontrolled, piercing him, burning him.

Her fingernails dug into his back. He pressed her against the counter, moved her legs apart with his, then aligned himself intimately with her. She felt too good. Too damn good...

Stop. Stop. His conscience went unheeded. Need demanded his attention now. Hot, driving need.

She quivered in his arms. Moaned. Pleaded. Yielded.

"Kiss me. Oh, please. Kiss me."

Her words were like ice water, a chilly reminder of their tenuous balancing act of fantasy and reality. How could he watch over her, keep her safe—and do his own job competently—if he let his emotions lead the way?

Dios. What was he doing? What had he done?

He stepped back, closing his eyes, unwilling to face her. His goodbye sounded abrupt, even to himself. He could only imagine how it sounded to her.

He swept up his jacket and headed for the door.

"Thank you for the use of your grandmother's ring," she called softly. "I'll be very careful with it."

It was the least of his worries.

Six

It was raining. J.D. propped a shoulder against the window frame of Misty's richly appointed library and stared at the yard, wondering if the rain was a sign that the wedding shouldn't take place. He glanced at his watch.

"It's thirty seconds later than the last time you looked," Judge Shaunnessey said, amusement in his voice. He'd been ordered by Misty, as had J.D., not to sit, so that they wouldn't wrinkle their garments. Patrick O'Halloran, J.D.'s best man and soon-to-be brother-in-law, was off seating guests in Misty's solarium, which would have been beautiful if not for the torrential downpour pounding the glass roof and dripping down the glass walls.

J.D. jammed his hands in his pockets and jangled his keys.

"I'd hate to see you before your execution," the judge commented.

"An execution would be less stressful to anticipate," J.D. responded. A lot weighed on his mind. Relief that the wait was over. Guilt at the sham he'd been forced to create. Anticipation of the marriage itself, even with the normal marital privileges off-limits. It had been difficult being publicly affectionate when they couldn't finish what they started each night. More difficult than he'd ever anticipated. Because of it, they'd avoided being alone since that night in her kitchen three weeks ago.

Tension was their constant companion. She'd even gotten mad at him last night after the rehearsal. Mad. All because he'd given her a pearl necklace to wear for the wedding. He hadn't expected stony silence to greet his gift, but it was what he'd gotten. She wouldn't even tell him why.

That was how they'd left things between them. And now they were to be married in less than fifteen minutes. That is, if she didn't stand him up.

Oh, he knew she was somewhere in Misty's house dressing in her finery, her dream gown, the one she'd imagined since she was a child. Yet another regret of his.

That didn't mean she'd go through with the wedding.

He reminded himself why they were doing this. Hastings had left Magnolia alone only because of the impending marriage, but his relationship with J.D. had undergone a change. Negotiations were tougher and more drawn out. Hastings exerted his power at every opportunity. J.D. would like nothing better than to respond in kind. The ball was not in his court, however. After all the months it had taken to set up the deal, he couldn't blow it now.

"She won't back out," the judge said, coming up beside J.D.

"I was not worried."

"Every groom worries. There are few moments in a man's life when he is more vulnerable than this one."

J.D. frowned. "Women really do wield the power, don't they?"

"It's a good thing they don't know how much."

"You think they don't?"

"Some do. Most don't."

"Does Misty?"

The judge looked at his own watch. "I think I'll just check that everything's on schedule. I'll be right back."

So, it didn't matter what your age or life experience, J.D. thought, the battle of the sexes continued to be waged, a tug-of-war in which physical strength didn't count.

He pushed back his shirt cuff and blew out a long breath. Ten minutes to go.

Maggie pressed a hand to her stomach. "I think I'm going to be sick."

"Good grief, Maggie. You'd think you were being sentenced to life in prison the way you've been acting," Jasmine said, smoothing the pale blue organdy fabric of her gown over her round belly. "Get a grip."

"Thank you so much for the sympathy."

"Why do you need sympathy? You're marrying the man you love, right? You've made the wedding dress of your dreams. Misty has created a beautiful setting for you, one you'll always remember. Stop whining."

"How come you're so testy, Jazz? You're always the soother."

"I'm on edge because you're on edge. Your mood is transferring to me. It's not good for me or the baby. So smile. Be happy. Because we want to be, too." She headed for an open door. "I have to go to the bathroom."

"Again? But—"

"When you're nine months' pregnant, you'll understand."

The door closed with a thump. Maggie flinched. She knew she was being a royal pain in the rear. Three weeks of ever-increasing tension had melded into a ball of fire in her stomach as day after day she and Diego played their parts and planned their wedding. He hadn't sat idly back and let her handle the wedding, either. She'd had to discuss everything with him. He'd even told her that he would be choosing her bouquet, which she hadn't even seen as yet.

Then last night he'd given her a beautiful pearl necklace as a wedding gift. When she'd asked him why he'd done it, he'd said it was on his list of responsibilities.

"What list?" she'd asked.

"The one in the bride magazine," he'd responded, pulling a folded and tattered piece of paper from his pocket, pointing to the list of groom's duties printed there. He'd obviously been using it as his bible to the wedding for all these weeks.

Because of it, he'd gotten her a necklace. Something else to be given back at the end of the charade.

At least the ring and the necklace could be boxed up and handed over. Did he expect she could do the same with the feelings that had changed and grown as they'd played out their game with the world?

She wished she could talk to him one more time. She needed his calmness right now, his assurance that they were doing what was necessary and right. She could picture him stretched out on a couch somewhere in the house, cool as a cloudburst, waiting for the ceremony to begin, everything under control.

At least her dress matched her dream. She'd appliquéd the winter white silk with lace, and hand-beaded the off-the-shoulder fitted bodice and train. A large fabric bow with a rose center rested at her waist in the back, hiding the hooks used to attach the chapel-length train. Twenty-five satin-covered buttons trailed her spine, her veil a cloud at the back of her head that floated almost to the floor.

The beading alone had taken a hundred and fifty hours—fifty of hers and one hundred by someone Misty had hired to help. Between making the gown and meeting the deadline for her magazine article, she hadn't had a second to breathe. It was no wonder she was a bundle of nerves. No one deserved a honeymoon more. Too bad she wasn't getting one, just one night at a honeymoon suite in an elegant hotel, which Patrick and Jasmine arranged, and Maggie and J.D. couldn't come up with an excuse to turn down. Yet another night of tension.

Misty swept into the room. "Here we go, hon. The bouquets

finally arrived. The delivery van was delayed because of the rain."

Maggie reached for the bouquet. "Oh, it's beautiful. Just beautiful." She pressed her face into the flowers and breathed their sweet fragrance. Tears stung as she realized that these, too, had come because of his list, not his heart.

"There's a card." Misty passed her an envelope.

Maggie set down the bouquet and opened the note. *Magnolia, The gardenias represent joy, the stephanotis's wish is for happiness, and the baby's breath honors a pure heart. These are you, as I see you. Diego.*

"Oh, God," she whispered. How can he write these things? Was he saying them to her or was he counting on others seeing his card and believing the charade?

"Don't you dare cry," Misty ordered. "You'll ruin your makeup."

"Blink your eyes a few times," Jasmine said as she came back into the room. "It's time for you to walk down that aisle."

"Already?"

Her sister's tone softened. "You'll feel better after it's over. It's what you want, isn't it, Maggie?"

"Yes," she whispered, suddenly more sure of anything than she'd ever been in her life. He wouldn't have gone to the lengths he had unless he cared. Really, deeply cared. "Yes, it's what I want."

Jasmine accepted her own bouquet from Misty, then watched as Maggie picked up hers. "You're the most beautiful bride I've ever seen. Chin up now. A nice smile. You're about to begin the adventure of your life."

Maggie smiled as she pushed her shoulders back and held her head high. Then like a warm summer breeze, calmness blanketed her. She was ready. More than ready. She hoped *he* was.

Ah, but she was beautiful, J.D. thought when he caught his first glimpse of her walking down the aisle on her nephew's arm. She was a fairy-tale princess in a cloud of billowy white. Her bright blue eyes shone like sapphires as they watched him in return, but her smile left her face by degrees the nearer she got to him. When he stepped forward and held out his arm for her to take she looked not at his face but at his chest.

"You got a new tuxedo," she whispered.

Of all the things he had anticipated she'd say, that one had never entered his mind. "Did you think I would wear my work clothes to my own wedding?" he snapped back in a fierce whisper, instantly regretting it when he watched her eyes fill with tears. He counted to five. He tried to smile at her. "You look like a princess."

Her mouth curved into a quavery smile, as well. "Thank you for the beautiful bouquet."

The judge cleared his throat quietly. "If we may begin."

The ceremony seemed endless to Maggie...and way too short. Words were repeated, music played, someone sang. She was only aware of Diego. Of the stark black of his tuxedo blended with the blue-and-black brocade of his vest, and the pristine white of his shirt. Of the new cologne he wore that wasn't familiar, yet hinted at his own particular scent. Of the strength of his hands as he slid a band of gold leaves that would entwine the diamond-and-sapphire daisy on her finger. She placed a plain gold band on his. Everything was a blur, and it made her want to weep.

She wanted to remember it all. The confusing, overwhelming emotions, the soft huskiness of his voice, the mix of fragrances of him and the flowers and women's perfume. She wanted him to hold her, closely, tenderly, infinitely. She wanted him to want more from her than friendship and desire. She wanted him to love her, as he was pledging before God and these thirty witnesses to do.

Because she loved him. Had loved him forever, she guessed. Would love him forevermore. She looked at his face as he focused on the judge, who was saying something about marriage being a partnership, a commitment, a joy.

A joy.

"You may kiss your bride."

The words penetrated the fog of her thoughts. She stood perfectly still as he cupped her face with both hands, smiled at her and gently tipped her head to the left.

There were no words to describe how his lips felt. There was only sound and sensation. Lightning and skyrockets and cymbals. Warmth and peace and liquid fire. So much light came from inside her, it blinded her to everything but him. She could have tasted him forever and still been hungry. But he ended the kiss and raised his head. They stared in awe at each other.

Then somewhere through it all she heard Jasmine say, "Oh, thank God. I've been in labor an hour. Patrick, I think you'd better get me to the hospital. My water broke ten minutes before the wedding."

Several minutes of unreality passed in a blur of pictures taken, transportation ordered and guests invited to enjoy the reception without the bride and groom.

"You should have stayed, Maggie," Jasmine said on the way to the hospital. "You should be at your reception celebrating. Dancing."

"We got through the ceremony," J.D. said, "and for that we thank you. But the reception will happen with or without us. She needs to be with you, Jasmine."

"You're family, too. You can be there."

"What, in delivery? I don't think so. But thanks for the offer. I think."

They must have been a comical sight, J.D. decided as they swept into the emergency room in tuxedos and wedding gown, trailing an orderly wheeling a not-very-tranquil pregnant woman through the halls of the hospital.

"I need to push. I really need to push," Jasmine kept saying.

"As soon as the doctor says," Patrick told her. He glanced at J.D., a multitude of unnamed emotions shining in his eyes.

J.D. felt the same flurry of emotions from Magnolia, in the way she squeezed his hand as they hurried along the corridor.

"Goodness gracious," exclaimed the nurse when they reached their destination. "Look at all the fancy dressers."

"I need to push," Jasmine told her through gritted teeth.

"Not yet, honey," she said cheerfully. "Let's get you out of your finery first. Which one's the husband? Okay, you can come along. You two can hang out in the waiting room for now."

"But I'm going to be there for the birth," Maggie said. "I took the classes. We're co-coaches."

The nurse's eyes sparkled. "Then I think maybe you'd best change into something else." She disappeared into a closet and returned bearing hospital greens. "Put these on. Room 218 is empty. Then you can join us in 221 when you're ready."

"I need you to unbutton me, Diego," Maggie said. "Come on."

His fingers felt as flexible as an arthritic's as he maneuvered the tiny buttons through their fabric loops, a chore that was aggravated by the fact she wouldn't, or couldn't, stand still.

"Take a few deep breaths, Magnolia," he said at last. "If you don't settle down I'm never going to manage this."

"I don't want to miss anything."

"I know. You won't."

"Jasmine had Matthew and Raine really fast, though. She's got the hips for it."

"Did you see them being born?"

"Her ex-husband wouldn't let me come in. How many more buttons?"

"Two. One. Okay, you're done."

He watched her shove the dress down and hop out of it. She swept it off the floor and turned from him to lay it across a chair. His eyes followed her movements. His mind stopped functioning.

Except for a frilly blue garter winking lasciviously at him from above her left knee, she was dressed all in white, from her satin high heels to her thigh-high embroidered stockings, to her skimpy briefs and strapless bra, from which her breasts threatened to spill out as she leaned over to step into the cotton pants the nurse had given her, the pearl necklace swaying freely.

She was perfection. Endless legs, well-toned thighs, a smooth, flat abdomen, generous curves, front and back, that were high and firm and mouthwatering.

And he'd been stupid enough to deny himself the right to enjoy it all.

He shook himself back to awareness. "I'll be in the waiting room."

"Come with me. Jazz wants you there, and I think Patrick needs the moral support. Did you see how white his face was? He's scared to death. You know what happened to his first wife."

"It seems like a private matter, Magnolia."

"You don't have to watch the baby come out. Just be there in a corner somewhere, in case you're needed. Patrick's your best friend."

He didn't remember agreeing but suddenly he was in the birthing room with everyone, a gown tied over his tuxedo.

He watched Maggie's excitement. He admired the way she took over when Patrick seemed ready to pass out. The pain that creased Jasmine's face seemed almost too much for a person to bear, yet between contractions she chatted and laughed, assuring Patrick she was fine.

"J.D.," she said suddenly after a long, excruciating contraction. "Come here a minute, please."

He couldn't have denied her anything. Maggie moved to make room for him.

"I'm glad you found the fire you were looking for," Jasmine said. "I found mine, too."

"I used to hate those cryptic little conversations you and Diego had when we all worked at the Carola together," Maggie said. "I still do."

"Tough. J.D., you helped my family get through the most

difficult time of our lives. The way you showed my children how to trust and love again was nothing short of a miracle. You were so good with them."

"I had gone through a similar experience, that's all."

"Being kidnapped by a parent—" She stopped to focus on a contraction before continuing. "It could have been years before we'd settled into a life together." She squeezed his hand. "I'm so glad Maggie has you. You're going to make a wonderful father."

He stepped back as the next contraction came fast on the heels of the last. He caught Magnolia's eye a moment as she gauged his reaction to her sister's words, then the doctor swept into the room.

"I hear you've been wanting to push, Jasmine. So, let's get going on the finale, shall we?"

J.D. stepped farther back, giving everyone room. He glanced at Patrick's face, damp with sweat, as if he were in labor himself.

He noted Jasmine's white knuckles as she squeezed his hands and bore down.

Magnolia had moved behind the doctor to look over his shoulder.

"I see the head!" She pressed her hands to her mouth. "Oh! It's through. Oh, how tiny."

"Tiny? It's enormous," Jasmine groaned.

"Here come the shoulders. And...the rest! Oh, look!"

A collective intake of breath silenced the room. Patrick lifted Jasmine a little higher to watch as the doctor held the baby up for inspection. A howl pierced the quiet.

"A boy," she said, turning toward her husband. "Oh, Patrick. A son. Our son."

A great deal of laughing and kissing and hugging followed, but what J.D. knew he'd remember most was the look on Patrick's face as the doctor passed him his son to place in his mother's arms.

Here was the miracle. Created out of love, born into a

strong, happy relationship, where no one would intentionally hurt anyone. The moment was almost too much to absorb.

Maggie watched the changing expressions on Diego's face. Love bloomed inside her, tempered by stark awareness of what she'd done by marrying a man without any promise of love or commitment or children. A man who saw her as a responsibility. And a liability? Could she change that?

She didn't see any cars when they returned to Misty's house an hour later. They were let in and walked hand in hand to the solarium, following the music from the four-piece band Misty had hired, which were playing something slow and sultry.

"I'll be damned," Diego said quietly.

Maggie followed his gaze as they stood in the doorway. Misty and Judge Shaunnessey were dancing—sort of. They were in each other's arms and swaying a little to the music. A piece of paper couldn't have been slid between their bodies.

"We should just leave," Maggie whispered.

But just then the judge spotted them and released Misty, although he still reached for her hand and held tight as she tried to tug free. "Here you are. Come in. Come in."

"Everyone finally gave up a little while ago," Misty said, her cheeks flushing even in the candlelight, the only light in the room other than the band's tiny lamps over their music stands. The rain had stopped but the sky was still cloudy, blocking the moon and stars. "Tell us everything. We're dying to know."

"Oh, it was all wonderful and beautiful and—"

"Humbling," Diego said.

"Yes." She smiled at him. "They've named him Charles Bryan O'Halloran. Chase, for short, and he's perfect."

"You can tell us more while you eat, but why don't you dance a while. I'll have a couple of dinner plates fixed for you. You can relax."

They stayed an hour, enjoying the company and the music, making a show of tossing the bouquet and garter to the two remaining guests. Then they changed clothes and were driven to the hotel where they were to spend their wedding night, the gift Patrick and Jasmine had arranged.

Although their suitcases had been delivered earlier and they were already in possession of the key, they were accompanied by a bellhop to the top floor of the small, luxurious hotel. He opened the door with a flourish.

Diego swept Maggie into his arms. "To keep away evil spirits," he said, the expert on wedding superstitions now that he'd studied the bride magazines.

Maggie laid her head on his shoulder and closed her eyes to enjoy the sensation of being carried across the threshold. As soon as the door closed, the playacting would end. She'd have to remember it wasn't real.

Misty had called ahead so the fireplace that divided the living room from the bedroom had been lit. The suite was sumptuously decorated, invitingly warm and private, yet with a view of San Francisco Bay that would be spectacular on a clear night. Diego set Maggie down so they could follow the bellhop around and listen to instructions. Their clothes had been put away for them; across the bed lay a beautiful red negligee and peignoir and matching red silk pajama bottoms and robe.

The bellhop left them staring at the bed.

"I didn't pack those," Maggie said, swallowing.

"You would have chosen white," he said with assurance, "but Misty knows I like red."

Maggie frowned at him. "How?"

"She asked. I told her."

"Oh." She set her bouquet that Misty had sneaked into the limo onto the bedside table, then swept up the garments to fold them, needing to get them out of sight. Then she went looking for her flannel nightgown and couldn't find it, just a note. *Shame on you, Maggie. This is your wedding night, not your fiftieth anniversary. Or was this some kind of joke on J.D.? Regardless, I'm burning these offensive garments for you. You'll thank me in the morning. Misty.*

"Apparently I have nothing else to wear," Maggie said,

tapping the paper against her lips. "It's either the red, completely see-through number or—"

"My shirt," Diego said, then proceeded to unbutton the garment he offered.

Seven

———

"No! I mean, not yet." Maggie cast a quick glance at the big, inviting bed. "I'm not ready to sleep. After everything that happened today, I may not even sleep at all."

J.D. hesitated, then he tipped her chin up with a finger. "You're exhausted. You've been burning the candle at both ends. Jasmine told me, but I saw for myself."

"I'm wide-awake," she protested.

"You're running on adrenaline. There's no one here for you to play games for now, *novia*. Let yourself unwind. Go take a long, hot bath, to start." He finished unbuttoning his shirt and slipped out of it, passing it to her. "After a good night's sleep, you'll be yourself again. I haven't recognized you lately."

She clutched the shirt to her as she tried not to stare at his chest. "What do you mean?"

"I mean you haven't fired some snappy insult at me in weeks. I miss it."

"You do?"

"Our relationship was built on verbal sparring, Magnolia. Did you think I'd want it to end?"

"I thought you needed me to act differently."

"For everyone else."

"Oh. I'm sorry."

He smiled at her. "You had a lot to occupy your mind. But now I want the old Magnolia back, okay?"

She was slow in answering. "Our relationship is bound to be different. The circumstances have changed it."

"I know. But we can still debate, can't we?" He brushed past her, picked up a fat candle and a book of matches, then disappeared into the bathroom.

Maggie heard him turn on the water. She peeked around the corner into the huge bathroom with its double-size whirlpool tub. He struck a match and lit the candle, then set it on the edge of the tub.

"It will take a while to fill." He turned off the lights as he passed by her so fast a breeze lifted her hair. "I will pour you a glass of the champagne that was left chilling for us."

She followed him into the living room, wondering about him. He'd just told her he wanted the old Maggie back, but she didn't know who this man was, either, this ultracheerful, talkative, clearly nervous man who usually seemed to move in slow motion. Maybe she should tell him that she wanted the old Diego back, too.

While waiting for the tub to fill, they stood at the window identifying landmarks as the clouds blew away. He talked constantly, and she kept eyeing him, curious. After a while he left her and she heard the water stop, then the sound of the whirlpool bubbling. She picked up her bouquet and carried it with her into the bathroom, where she set it next to the candle so that she could enjoy the fragrance in the steamy room.

"Thank you for the beautiful note you sent with the flowers." She dipped her hand in the water to test the temperature. "I'm sorry I got mad at you last night."

"Why did you?"

"Because I didn't have a gift for you." The lie came easily.

"I could still give you a gift. The most personal gift I know how to give."

He didn't pretend to misunderstand her. But until this assignment was over and everyone, including himself, was safe, he couldn't take advantage of her willingness or his desire to make the marriage any more real. He couldn't think about the long-term, only the here and now. He had to put his job first—the job he'd almost lost, even after all he'd invested in it. He was doubly obligated to succeed now.

"You'd know I was lying if I told you I wasn't tempted," he told her, stepping back. "I've wanted you for a long time. I can't hide that from you. But the reasons for our marriage haven't changed. It's just *less* dangerous now."

"Tell me why you think so, Diego. I'm trying to understand. It's getting harder for me to understand when I'm starting to feel really married."

"Don't. There's much more to Hastings than I can tell you. I asked you to trust me on that. I know it's asking a lot, but I need that from you."

"But what does it have to do with you? What does he have to do with your life? And mine?"

"You know I can't—"

"Are you in trouble, Diego?"

He read the suspicion in her eyes. Should he tell her? Could she keep her face schooled around Hastings? Could he take the chance?

"Why won't you answer me?" she asked. "I'm your wife now. What affects you, affects me."

"When I can, I will. You won't have too long to wait."

She frowned. "Does that mean our marriage will be over soon?"

"If I could have given you a time frame, we could have just pretended to be engaged." He turned abruptly. "Your water is cooling."

J.D. shut the door behind him. Toying with the unfamiliar ring on his finger, he glanced at the bed. He allowed his fantasies free rein for a minute before he folded back the bedding.

He killed more time by phoning the hospital to check on Jasmine and the baby, feeling like a real member of a family having the right to call and check.

Deciding there was no reason he couldn't wear the pajamas and robe Misty had left for him, he changed into them, then settled in a chair in the bedroom. As he sipped his champagne, he thought about how much his life had changed in the past month. Contentment drifted over him. He'd accomplished his primary goal of keeping Magnolia safe from Hastings. Even unwilling, she could have been well established in Hastings's penthouse by now, a slave to his crude pleasures until he tired of her.

J.D. shoved thoughts of Hastings aside, and recaptured his earlier contentment. It had been a good day, even if it hadn't gone exactly according to plan.

He turned his head when the bathroom door opened. Knowing she hadn't spotted him in the dimly lit bedroom, he watched as she hung up her skirt and sweater and put away her lingerie. Then she headed toward the living room.

"I'm here," he said, rising and walking toward her. His shirt covered her to mid-thigh. The sleeves were rolled to just below her elbows. Lucky shirt.

"Spyin', honey?"

Ah, good, his Magnolia was back. "I'd almost fallen asleep."

"Really? I'm wide-awake. How about a game of cards or something?"

"Cards."

She hooked a finger under his robe sash. "Sure. How about strip poker? Could be a really fast game. I'm wearing one item and you've only got on two. You look nice in red, by the way."

"I cheat."

"Fine with me. I'd planned on losin', anyway."

He heard the tension in her voice. The bath hadn't relaxed her at all. She was riding a roller coaster of emotion that only sleep and time would bring to a stop. Although…maybe there was something else he could do for her, after all.

"How much sleep did you get last night?" he asked.

"A couple of hours, I guess. Why?"

"Why don't you get in bed and I'll give you a back rub. It'll help you relax."

"I'd rather play strip poker." Maggie grumbled all the way to the bed. "You're going to have to learn how to have fun. You take life far too seriously."

"I'll take it under consideration."

"I suppose I have to leave the shirt on, too. Wouldn't want to tempt you too much, now, would we?" Without waiting for an answer, she stretched out facedown in the middle of the bed, giving him room to sit beside her. Loving him was not going to be easy. Loving him and not being able to show it was going to be impossible, especially on the terms he'd established. And if they had only a little time…

She couldn't stop a groan from escaping when he kneaded her shoulders.

"*Dios*. Your muscles have no give whatsoever. Relax."

"I'm trying," she said, her jaw clenched.

After a few minutes, she heard him mutter a few words in Spanish. "Maybe you should take off the shirt, after all," he said, rolling off the bed. "I'll be back in a minute."

She understood that he expected her to strip and cover up by the time he returned, so she cooperated. She pulled off the shirt, not bothering to unbutton it and slid facedown again, pulling the sheet up respectably to her waist, trying not to anticipate too much.

The bed shifted under her as he returned. She held her breath. His hands were cool and slick with lotion that he spread across her shoulders and down her back, kneading her muscles, drawing little sounds of pleasure-pain from her.

"That's better," he said, his voice as soothing as the massage.

After a while, she felt his hands glide down her arms. His fingers massaged hers, one by one, then his thumbs pressed her palms. Her arms turned rubbery. For a few minutes he massaged her back again, straying a little lower each time, until she felt the sheet drift down and his hands, his large, talented hands, knead her bottom.

She was afraid even to breathe, that to disrupt the moment by the tiniest indication of what she was feeling would end the pleasure. Maybe he thought she was asleep.

She felt his hands stroke her thighs, then a gentle tug to move her legs apart. The bed jostled as he knelt between her legs and pulled one foot up to massage for a while, then the other. He slid his hands back up her legs, pushing, pressing, stroking. His fingers feathered the inside of her thighs.

"Easy," he said softly as he touched her intimately and she jumped.

Gentle fingertips stroked her, drawing her essence, teasing her until she squirmed. The core of her pounded with a thundering cadence.

He leaned over her, his hands bracketing her shoulders, his mouth close to her ear, making her shiver. "Roll over."

Because he still knelt between her legs, she had to maneuver hers around him as she turned. He pushed them wider apart, leaving her vulnerable...and wanting him. He wasn't even touching her. Anticipation alone drummed her flesh rhythmically. His gaze never strayed from her face. She didn't know what he saw in her expression because she'd never felt anything like this before.

"Kiss me, Diego. Please, I think I'm going to die if you don't."

He threaded his fingers into her hair, holding her still as he settled his mouth against hers, a lingering pressure that deepened and built and thrilled. She hadn't imagined the passion earlier. She hadn't fantasized that it was better than reality. His lips were as soft, but more demanding. He tasted dark and hot and mysterious. And he knew exactly when to retreat, when to press, when to tease, when to satisfy. How did that song go? A kiss is just a kiss? That songwriter had never been kissed by James Diego Duran.

They moaned together, their mouths opening, tongues seeking, in a kiss that lasted longer than earthly time could measure, then he raised up and started a slow massage of her thighs, every so often letting his thumbs meet at the juncture to tease and stroke and glide slickly up and down until she writhed and begged. The pad of his thumb sought the hard center that ached, swirling lightly until her whole body tensed.

Leaving her hovering at the precipice, he leaned over her, sliding his hands behind her waist and lifting her until her back arched and her head dropped back. He traced a path around each nipple with his tongue, laved the plump flesh of each breast before finally settling on a hard peak that begged for him to suckle and cherish. A thunderbolt flashed to her womb, bringing with it an explosion beyond anything of her experience. Then just as it started to fade and she was finding air to breathe again, he cupped her intimately with his hand, pressing with the heel, letting his fingers dance. She arched shamelessly higher, pleaded with him to hurry, succeeding only in his defiantly slowing his pace. Again and again he let her almost reach the peak before pulling back, until one touch was all that was necessary. And what followed was indescribably beautiful and glorious, and everything that any poet had ever tried to describe. A sustained, fiery explosion like a star burning itself out after a millennium of brilliance.

In a haze of semiconsciousness, she was vaguely aware of him pulling the sheet over her as he rolled off the bed. She turned her head in time to see him slip back into the robe he'd discarded a while ago.

"Where are you going?" she asked as he walked away.

"Go to sleep, Magnolia."

Her mouth dropped open. *Go to sleep, Magnolia?* Furious, the tension back in full force, she scrambled out of bed, yanked his shirt over her head and followed him.

"What was all that about?" she demanded to know, wedging herself between him and the bar before he could pour what appeared to be Scotch into a glass.

His jaw hardened. He moved her aside. "You're supposed to be relaxed now. Go back to bed before you tense up again."

She sputtered as he splashed the amber liquid into a glass. "I don't get to return the favor?"

J.D. eyed her as he downed the fiery drink, then plunked the empty glass onto the bar top. He swiped the back of his hand across his mouth. "I don't need anything."

The hurt in her eyes sliced him like a dull knife.

"Damn you, Diego. Damn you." She turned from him and walked unsteadily to stand at the window. Silence hung between them a long while. "It figures," she said finally, sounding resigned. "Now that it's after midnight and our wedding day is officially over, the clouds are gone. Everything's status quo again, right? Everything. I knew it wasn't going to be real. I just thought…well, I guess it doesn't matter."

He curled his fingers into fists as she rested her cheek against the cold plate glass. He burned for her—physically, mentally, emotionally. Whoever had taken her virginity hadn't destroyed her innocence as he just had.

"Magnolia—"

"You're always giving to me." Turning toward him she propped her shoulders and the back of her head against the window as she crossed her arms. "You never let me give you anything in return. Do you have any idea how that makes me feel?"

She walked a slow path his way. He could see her trying to make a mask of her face, but she was as readable as she'd always been.

"You married me to protect me. You fixed my door and put in a security system for which you won't let me repay you. You gave me your grandmother's rings to wear. You paid for most of the wedding. You not only helped plan everything but you took over a lot of the details. Then when I was tired and stressed, you ran my bath for me, set a mood with a candle, gave me a back rub, made love to my body, if not my mind."

He would have questioned that last phrase except that he didn't want to encourage the conversation.

"You did all that for me, and now you won't let me give you anything in return. Nothing. What am I, inconsequential? Just a prop? You'd do the same for any woman?"

"No." He couldn't stop the denial, any more than he could stop himself from taking hold of her shoulders and making her look him in the eye. "I care about you. I always have. You know that."

"Not enough. If you cared enough you would trust me. You would tell me why. You would answer my questions. You would let me give to you as you give to me. I am nothing. No one."

When she set her hands lightly at his waist, desire rekindled instantly deep inside him.

"Maybe because you know I'm not as experienced as you," she said, "you think I couldn't bring you the same level of pleasure. That may even be true. But I guarantee you I'd give all I have in me to give."

She leaned forward and pressed her lips to the base of his throat. He sucked in a quick, hard breath.

"If I let you, Magnolia," he said, struggling to resist her, "the fact we haven't consummated the marriage is merely a technicality."

She stared at him as she untied the sash of his robe and slid her arms around him. "I don't know why the legalities are so important to you, but I do understand that they are. I'm willing to keep it all legal. For now. Will you let me? Will you come back to bed and let me make love to you in return? Will you allow me that pleasure?"

He'd made some hard decisions in his life. This one ranked higher than any other. "It would change too much between us," he said quietly and watched her put more than physical distance between them.

"I'm trying hard to admire your integrity." She trailed a hand along the back of the sofa, her tone of voice neutral. "And if I felt you considered me your friend and partner,

PLAY
SILHOUETTE'S
LUCKY HEARTS
GAME

AND YOU GET

- ★ FREE BOOKS
- ★ A FREE GIFT
- ★ AND MUCH MORE

**TURN THE PAGE AND
DEAL YOURSELF IN** →

PLAY "LUCKY HEARTS" AND GET...

★ **Exciting Silhouette Desire® novels—FREE**

★ **PLUS a Lovely Simulated Pearl Drop Necklace—FREE**

THEN CONTINUE YOUR LUCKY STREAK WITH A SWEETHEART OF A DEAL

1. Play Lucky Hearts as instructed on the opposite page.
2. Send back this card and you'll receive brand-new Silhouette Desire® novels. These books have a cover price of $3.50 each, but they are yours to keep absolutely free.
3. There's no catch. You're under no obligation to buy anything. We charge nothing — ZERO — for your first shipment. And you don't have to make any minimum number of purchases — not even one!
4. The fact is thousands of readers enjoy receiving books by mail from the Silhouette Reader Service. They like the convenience of home delivery…they like getting the best new novels months before they're available in stores…and they love our discount prices!
5. We hope that after receiving your free books you'll want to remain a subscriber. But the choice is yours — to continue or cancel, anytime at all! So why not take us up on our invitation, with no risk of any kind. You'll be glad you did!

NOT ACTUAL SIZE

*This lovely necklace will add glamour to your most elegant outfit! Its cobra-link chain is a generous 18" long, and its lustrous simulated cultured pearl is mounted in an attractive pendant! Best of all, it's **absolutely free**, just for accepting our no-risk offer.*

SILHOUETTE'S

With a coin— scratch off the silver card and check below to see what we have for you.

YES! I have scratched off the silver card. Please send me all the free books and gift for which I qualify. I understand that I am under no obligation to purchase any books, as explained on the back and on the opposite page.

225 CIS A7DY **(U-SIL-D-03/97)**

NAME

ADDRESS   APT.

CITY   STATE   ZIP

Twenty-one gets you 4 free books, and a free simulated pearl drop necklace

Twenty gets you 4 free books

Nineteen gets you 3 free books

Eighteen gets you 2 free books

Offer limited to one per household and not valid to current Silhouette Desire® subscribers. All orders subject to approval.

© 1990 HARLEQUIN ENTERPRISES LIMITED.   **PRINTED IN U.S.A.**

DETACH AND MAIL CARD TODAY

THE SILHOUETTE READER SERVICE™: HERE'S HOW IT WORKS

Accepting free books places you under no obligation to buy anything. You may keep the books and gift and return the shipping statement marked "cancel". If you do not cancel, about a month later we'll send you 6 additional novels, and bill you just $2.90 each plus 25¢ delivery per book and applicable sales tax, if any.* That's the complete price–and compared to cover prices of $3.50 each–quite a bargain! You may cancel at any time, but if you choose to continue, every month we'll send you 6 more books, which you may either purchase at the discount price…or return to us and cancel your subscription.

*Terms and prices subject to change without notice. Sales tax applicable in N.Y.

perhaps I could forgive your masculine stubbornness. But you don't seem to recognize that I also have integrity. And pride. And honor. I hate that you take all that from me in some irrational need to be the man, with a capital *M*.''

"I do not mean to do that, Magnolia.''

"Whether or not you mean to doesn't negate the fact that you do. I'm telling you that we could sleep together—literally, sleep—in that very large, very inviting bed in the next room. On my honor. But you don't believe that, do you?''

It was as neat a debate as J.D. had ever heard, one that would make him seem petty and immature indeed if he didn't accept the challenge. To hide a threatening smile, he looked at the floor for a few moments. When he resettled his gaze on her, he let himself recall the womanly body hidden by his shirt, the taste of her nipples, the gently curving line of her waist and hip and thighs, the firm flesh of her rear...her uninhibited response to his touch, to his need to bring her pleasure. She couldn't question again whether she'd climaxed. Not even "sort of.''

The echo of his own arrogance resonated in his head. Did he sound like that to her? If so, she had a right to chastise him. Although, it was merely the truth—

"I'm going to bed,'' she said, raw weariness coating her words. "I assume you'll be out here.''

"I could use a good night's sleep myself. I don't think I'll get it on the sofa.''

Maggie blinked away her shock. She watched him switch off the lamps and check the fire. He moved to the doorway.

"Coming?'' he asked.

She dug deep to toss an impudent smile his way as she passed in front of him and headed to the bed. "I did. Twice.'' She looked over her shoulder and fluttered her eyes at him. "Thank you.''

He laughed and the tension was broken. They climbed into bed from opposite sides. Maggie didn't hover on the edge; neither did she stray too far toward the middle. They lay in silence a few minutes, each staring at the ceiling.

"If I started shivering," she said into the quiet, "what would you do?"

He turned his head toward her. "The fire is blazing, Magnolia."

"Hypothetically."

"Ah. Hypothetically, it would be my responsibility to warm you. I believe it was one of the vows I took today. Yesterday."

"Love, honor and provide heat?" she queried.

"Rings a bell. My memory of the ceremony is a little hazy." He rolled onto his side. "Are you cold?"

"Hypothetically."

"And this is your way of proving your integrity to me, right? By tempting me even further?"

"It would make for a truly memorable wedding night, don't you think, Diego? The Night of Passionate Resistance."

"The Endless Night of..." He sighed. "Well, come here, then. Let's hypothetically warm you up."

Spooned together, they faced the fire. Maggie wriggled until she found the perfect spot against him, the one that made him groan because he couldn't hide his body's response to her nearness.

"Sorry," she whispered as he clamped a hand against her hip, stilling her.

"I've been in this condition so much for the past month, it feels like the norm," he said, his warm breath dusting her ear, making her skin rise in bumps. "Do you realize how often you amend rules to suit you, Magnolia?"

"I call it being flexible."

Humor sugared the lyrically foreign words that rolled off his tongue and she relaxed against him. She would get him to change his mind about letting her return the pleasure he'd given her. Sooner rather than later, she hoped. She'd find the right time to tell him she loved him, too, at a time when he would be receptive to hearing the words and not dismiss them out of hand. Until then, they could get to know each other better.

"Good night," she said softly, unapologetically happy. She

wanted him to sleep so that she could stay awake all night and savor being in his arms.

"Sweet dreams."

A long time later, when his arm lay heavily across her waist as he slept, she turned slowly to face him. He had the dearest face. So fierce at times, so full of humor at others. He was everything she'd ever wanted in a lifetime mate—protective, kind and intelligent, with a small dose of arrogance and cynicism tossed in for interest. As a lover, he was generous and overwhelming. As a friend, he was loyal and committed, a much better giver than receiver. She'd have to teach him that it was all right to accept the gifts he was offered.

With the lightest of touches, she brushed a fallen lock of hair from his forehead, hesitating when he stirred. He rolled onto his back, pulling her along and tightening his hold.

"Can't you sleep?" he mumbled, stroking her back absently.

"I just needed to change position," she said. But he'd gone back to sleep already. She snuggled closer, sliding her leg between his, loving the feel of his skin beneath her cheek, loving the scent of him and the heat and the strength. Although she continued to fight it, the need to sleep overpowered the need to memorize this whole night in his arms, an occurrence that wouldn't happen again anytime soon, not if he had anything to say about it.

Her eyes drifted shut. She blinked them open. They closed again.

"Sleep now, *novia*." His voice, husky and mesmerizing, lulled her along with him into slumber. "Be at peace."

She didn't fight any longer.

Eight

"Are you planning on spending the whole day in bed, lazybones?"

The words took a left turn inside Maggie's head and pushed at her eyes, forcing them open. Diego came into focus as he sat beside her on the bed. The enticing fragrance of really good coffee had her sniffing the air. Her gaze settled on the steaming mug he tipped to his mouth.

"There wouldn't be another of those nearby, would there?"

He leaned across her and lifted a matching mug from the nightstand. "Sweet and light," he said, passing it her way as soon as she pulled herself up.

"You're in serious danger of spoiling me rotten. There'll be no one to blame but you," she said, smiling at him before she closed her eyes and breathed the rising vapors, then took an appreciative swallow. "Ahhh. French roasted heaven."

After leaning into the pillows he stacked behind her, she decided it was patently unfair that he looked so fresh and appealing in his hunter green cable-knit sweater and black slacks while she sported a wrinkled, oversize shirt and sleep-mussed hair. Except that he also looked irritated or something and was trying not to show it.

"What's wrong?"

His glance slid away. He sipped again. "Nothing."

Maggie frowned. "How long have you been awake?"

Why, Magnolia, I've been awake all night, thanks to you. Either her sweet, tempting butt had been pressed against him, or her leg was thrown over the top of him, her knee holding him hostage, or, as was the case an hour ago, her hand was plopped into his lap, blanketing the hard length of him as he pulsed and yearned for her.

Only knowing she was sound asleep and not in the least aware of what she was doing had saved him from waking her up, shoving the fabric barrier out of the way and letting her return the favor, as she'd called it.

He didn't know how long they'd lain like that. He'd been pulled from sleep by a dream so erotic, so graphic, he'd been choking for air, the tentacles of lust slithering over and around his body to tighten and tease. And when consciousness fired the dream out of a cannon to end it, he'd discovered her twined with him, his hips rising instinctively to enjoy the unconsciously arousing grip of her hand. After a long time he'd loosened her hold, and headed for the shower.

"Diego?"

He stood and moved away, keeping his back to her as he set his mug on the hearth and poked at the fire. "What?"

"I asked how long you've been awake."

"Half an hour or so."

"Oh, good. I thought you'd been waiting on me. What time is it?"

"Two."

"In the afternoon? Are you serious?"

"No. I'm just playing with your mind."

She sighed. "Well, don't do that. At least not until I'm fully awake."

He turned toward her and grinned. "It's actually two-fifteen."

"Well, that's better." Maggie yawned. Holding the cup still, she stretched languorously, one arm reaching for the ceiling. "I have never slept so well in all my life. How about you?"

"I slept...hard."

"Me, too. I dreamed a lot. I just can't remember any of them." She watched his eyes blaze a trail along her body as she pushed the bedcovers aside and swung her legs around to set her feet on the floor. After setting her coffee on the table, she shoved her fingers through her hair, loosening the tangles.

"I called the hospital," he said, meeting her gaze as she grabbed the edge of the mattress with both hands and leaned forward. "Jasmine and Patrick are taking the baby home later on. She said if we came by today, they wouldn't answer the door, but that tomorrow we would be welcome. She's still irritated that we would accept only one night here instead of a week, but she figures since we actually did resist sleeping together before the wedding, we won't want to leave our bedroom until at least tomorrow."

"There's a lovely fantasy." She pushed herself off the bed to approach him. "I liked sleeping with you. And I'm pleased to tell you that you don't snore."

He watched her mosey his way. Magnolia in his shirt was the sexiest thing he'd ever seen. "Neither do you," he said as she stopped before him, her lips curving upward.

"I'd been worried about that."

"I figured."

She hadn't fastened the top two buttons, and a third had pulled open during the night, giving him a glimpse now of sloping white flesh. She smelled of spices and arousal—as well she should. They'd kept each other in that state all night, even asleep.

"You're a tempting package," he said, eyeing her.

"Misty's been giving me lessons."

"Excuse me?"

She set her hands at his waist, grinning lazily. "She said since my mother wasn't here to instruct me on the facts of life, she would."

His brows raised. "How generous. Did you learn anything?"

"It was my bachelorette party and everyone else had gone home. We were tipsy. I do remember giggling a lot. Some of her ideas were so exotic. And I do recall thinking I would be embarrassed to try a few of them."

"Like what?"

"Oh, no. You're not gonna get me to tell you the secrets of the ages. You'd accuse me of teasin' you, honey."

He slid two fingers under the open vee of her shirt and stroked the valley between her breasts, letting his fingers drift farther apart with each glide. Her flesh quivered.

"Just one little secret," he said, distracting her by moving his hand across her breast until the hard tip rested against his palm.

"Not even under the threat of death," she said seriously.

"Aw, come on. Be a sport."

She shifted closer as he thumbed her nipple. "Misty said," she whispered soberly, "that if I put my fingers like so—" she demonstrated as she talked "—on this part of your anatomy, you could last all night."

He choked out her name.

"At least, I think that's where she meant. We didn't have a model or anything. And I was *this close* to being drunk."

"Don't pinch. *Dios,* Magnolia."

"Now all I want to do is test the theory." She stepped back, pleased with her new power.

One side of his mouth tipped up. He leaned close. "What makes you think I need any help to last all night?"

She swallowed.

"Breakfast will be delivered in about fifteen minutes," he said, turning away. "I'll pack while you shower. We have already stayed beyond checkout time."

Maggie reached the bathroom door, then turned around. "I wonder if Judge Shaunnessey spent the night with Misty."

"Looked like a possibility. Why?"

"He's so much better suited to her than those young studs she has at her beck and call. She needs someone like him. I wonder what keeps them apart."

"She doesn't think she's good enough for him," he said as he pulled a suitcase out of the closet.

"That's dumb. You can overcome anything if you love each other."

As she closed the door, she was still making noises about it. He unzipped the bag and flipped the lid open. He stared into the empty suitcase, thinking how his father could tell her a thing or two about romantic idealism and how it only results in pain.

They hiked the stairs to her apartment an hour later. He inserted the key and opened the door. No high-pitched warning greeted him. Alert, he set down the suitcase.

"Do you remember if you set the alarm?" he asked low and hushed. He felt her tense behind him.

"Of course I set the alarm."

"Are you positive?"

"Well...no. I assume I did since I always—"

"Who else has access?"

"No one. I didn't give the code to Jasmine because she wasn't out and about, anyway."

"Wait here." He shut the door as she was still speaking and drew his weapon. Nothing seemed out of place in the living room. He crept into her bedroom, moved into the connecting bathroom and through to what would become his room, where the boxes of his personal belongings he'd brought over a couple of days ago awaited him. After replacing the gun in his ankle holster, he returned to her just as she shoved the door open.

"You must have forgotten to set it," he said.

"No way. You've scared me enough that I've been really careful."

"Come in and take a close look. You'd see things that I wouldn't." He reached past her for the suitcase, then stepped aside.

"Are you still worried about Brendan?" she asked. "I thought our marriage was supposed to end any threat from him."

"When an alarm that should be set, isn't, I worry. Period."

Maggie didn't budge.

"No one's here," he said, cocking his head at her, curious.

She picked imaginary lint off her sleeve. "Aren't you afraid of evil spirits if you don't carry me over the threshold here, too?"

He rested his arms against the doorjamb and grinned at her. Feeling a rush of heat flood her face, Maggie scowled. "Forget it. Just forget it. You were the superstitious—"

He swept her into his arms as she started across the threshold. Their faces were inches apart. She looked at his mouth. He backed up a step to kick the door shut.

"Turn the dead bolt," he said.

She reached behind him to do so, then slid both arms around his neck. After a minute, he set her down and turned away to pick up the suitcase. "Have you cleared space in your room for my stuff?"

Hope leapt from his words to her heart. "You mean you'll be sleeping with me, after all?"

"I'll be sleeping in the second bedroom. But our things need to commingle for appearances' sake."

She refused to let her disappointment show as she moved past him and headed for her bedroom, knowing he followed. Her gaze swept her bedroom once, twice. She opened the jewelry box on her dresser and peered in.

J.D. leaned against the doorjamb and watched her move around the room that was so much like her, delicate, feminine, traditional. Traditional. It continued to surprise him, the old-fashioned side of her, the nester, the homemaker. He glanced at the collection of antique perfume bottles, a shimmering rainbow of crystal reflected in the framed oval mirror on which they rested. Her bed was blanketed with a handmade quilt, her own creation undoubtedly.

Everything was tidy…and frilly enough to make him feel like a boxer at a tea party. Even the telephone on the lace-covered nightstand was feminine, all white and gold and—

He zeroed in on it. Bugged? Had someone managed to get in and bug the apartment? *Dios.* What had they talked about? Had they said anything— Yes. Too much. He had to get her out of here and get Callahan in to sweep for the electronic surveillance that could not only undo his patient efforts of the past year and a half, but put both himself and Magnolia at risk.

"We should go to the grocery store before we get too involved here," he said. He'd have to use his cellular phone, even though he hated to. Cellulars were so vulnerable. "I'll meet you outside in a minute." He had a one-minute head start on her, he figured. Little enough time to make a call before she caught up to him.

"I stocked up. There's plenty…" Maggie's words drifted off as she heard him hurrying down the steps like an Olympic runner going for the gold. What in the world had gotten into him? Was he afraid to be alone with her in her bedroom?

She ran a brush through her hair, then followed him, happy to be sharing her life with him, even if he was a puzzle. She punched the four-digit code into the alarm panel and thought about him some more. Maybe *because* he was a puzzle, she amended mentally.

J.D. stretched an arm along the back of the couch as he swigged an ice-cold beer. They'd worked hard all evening, rearranging her room and his. She'd left her sewing machine and dress form in his room, but the computer now took up a corner of the living room so that he could open the sleeper-sofa without shoving furniture around each night. They'd talked about her magazine articles that she wanted to sell as a book, the designing she'd started to do for Misty's lingerie company, what her last semester course schedule would entail starting next week, how much kidding they'd both be in for tomorrow night when they went back to work. They made plans to see the baby tomorrow morning. He liked being included automatically, not asked if he wanted to go. They were a couple now, a team, a partnership.

He'd asked her to continue wearing the pager she'd been given supposedly by Patrick and Jasmine, so that he could track her down, if necessary. Because she hadn't seem offended by the request, he planned to get her a cellular phone, as well.

Lulled by the sound of water running as she showered, he leaned his head back to rest on the top of the sofa, content. Callahan had found no bugs. She'd just forgotten to turn on the alarm, that was all.

The water stopped. He imagined her drying off, rubbing lotion or dusting powder or whatever over her velvety skin.

"Bathroom's free," she called from behind her bedroom door.

He pushed himself up and meandered through his room and on into the bathroom, still steamy and fragrant. He wondered if she'd be in bed by the time he got out.

After a few minutes, he heard the bathroom door open.

"Just passing through," she said. "I'm going to make up your bed."

The shower curtain blew toward him and clung to his thigh as she hurried past. He ducked his head under the stream to rinse out the shampoo and cover his laugh. She was so damn obvious. What was he going to do with her?

Maggie contemplated her reflection in her cheval glass. She didn't want to be too obvious, but Misty had confiscated her flannel nightgown and cozy robe, leaving few options for bed wear. A handful of seriously sexy pieces of lingerie filled a dresser drawer, but she couldn't be so blatant.

So, what should she wear for the after-shower, before-bed hour or so?

From a hanger she plucked one of his shirts, a mostly white one with blue pinstripes, button-down collar and long sleeves with cuffs that she rolled four times. A pair of fleecy white slouchy socks served as slippers. She spritzed a little perfume between her breasts and buttoned the shirt to that spot, then fastened one more so he couldn't accuse her of being a tease.

The shower stopped just as she fluffed two pillows and propped them on his bed. She scurried into the living room, shutting his door behind her and flying onto the couch. She tried to assume a casual pose. She changed positions a few times, then picked up a magazine and settled. Her heart thundered, which made focusing on any typewritten words impossible. She flipped pages without seeing anything.

He moved on silent feet into the living room, but she knew he was there. Casually, she shifted her gaze to wander up him, past the sweatpants and T-shirt, to catch the intense look in his eyes.

"That shirt looks a hell of a lot better on you than on me, Magnolia."

"You don't mind? I didn't ask—"

"What's mine is yours, *novia.*" J.D. sat beside her. He eyed a package sitting on the coffee table. "You still haven't opened it."

"You can. It's for both of us."

"But it's from *your* mother."

"Who didn't see any value in attending either Jasmine's or my wedding. Patrick offered to fly her here for both occasions. Even a free trip didn't interest her." She pushed herself up and headed for the kitchen.

"When did you last see her?"

"I went to New Orleans on vacation three years ago. I had this absurd hope that it would somehow be different between us. Can I get you anything?"

He lifted the package into his lap. The address was penned in a strong, neat hand. "What are you having?"

"Tea."

Setting the package down, he joined her in the kitchen. "I'll make myself some coffee."

"I can do that."

"You don't have to wait on me, Magnolia."

She leaned against the counter and crossed her arms. "But I like to."

"If it makes you happy, you can cut me another slice of apple pie."

"Do you want it heated?"

He watched his shirt hike a couple of inches up her thighs as she leaned into the refrigerator to pull out the homemade pie she'd taken out of the freezer and baked earlier. *Who needs heat?* he wondered. "Heated's fine."

"Ice cream?"

"Okay." He dumped coffee beans into the grinder, releasing their fragrance with a brief, noisy whirl. When their food was ready, they returned to the living room. He took a bite of pie and ice cream, complimented her on it, as he had earlier, then swallowed some coffee. "What do you mean that you hoped it would be different with your mother?"

She blew into the mug she held with both hands. "Are you sure you want to hear this?"

"Of course."

She tucked her legs under her. "My mother was forty-four years old when I was born. By then, she'd been married three times. Since then, she's been married three more times. She's in great shape for her age. That's part of the problem. She's always wanted to seem younger than her age—substantially younger. She's had two face-lifts that I know of, tummy tucks, the works. After each divorce she has herself redone and starts hunting again."

"She sounds desperate."

She shrugged. "In a way having Jazz and me when she was older made it easier for her to lie about her age, which she does regularly. Not that anyone cares but her. But each new husband was younger than the one before. My father was ten years younger.''

"You've never mentioned your father before.''

"I don't know where he is, or even if he's alive. He only stuck it out a couple of years before my mother drove him away. He remarried and had a new family.'' She blew on her tea again. "In the beginning I saw him occasionally, but I think his wife was jealous so she discouraged any relationship. I accepted it because Jazz was there to keep things okay. But she got married and moved here when I was twelve.''

"That's a difficult age to have anything major happen.'' He waited as she drank carefully. "Tell me about your stepfathers. Did they treat you all right?''

"Meaning, did any of them abuse me? No. One of them was pretty creepy, though. I made sure I wasn't ever alone with him. When I was sixteen I left home and came here to live with Jazz and her first husband until I graduated from high school. I've been on my own ever since.'' She sipped again, taking her time. "None of the men in my mother's life had any ambition. Jazz and I have different opinions on this subject. She says Mom always needed a man to take care of her. I say she never married anyone who *could* take care of her.''

He set his plate aside. "Is that important to you? That a man takes care of a woman?''

"I think a husband and wife should contribute equally, in whatever roles they're suited for. But my mother's husbands never did much. She was the one who worked all the time, mostly swing shift, so I never saw her. I hated it. We moved a lot, too. It was hard enough not having my mother around, but I kept having to make new friends. My children will have what I didn't.''

Her expression seemed carved in marble—defiant, determined, and with a warrior's unwavering conviction to a cause, even as feminine as she was. He hadn't imagined this side of her.

"What will be different, Magnolia?''

"My children will know stability, and have a sense of place. I've worked hard to develop a career where I can work at home so that I can share their lives. They won't ever wonder if their mother loves them."

She stopped abruptly, as if she'd revealed too much. "She meant well. At times. I guess."

He had no sympathy for people who mean well. "How does all of this connect with your goal of being married by age thirty?"

"I just want to be young enough to enjoy my children."

He angled her direction. "So you want kids right away."

"I figure that by the time you and I get an annulment or whatever and I find someone else and get married for real, another year or so will have gone by." Curious at the way his jaw tightened, she decided to test his reaction further. She switched on the Louisiana drawl. "I'm really, really ready for marriage and everything that it entails. I'm s'posedly at my sexual peak, you know, honey."

Oh, yes, that drew a response, she thought, as his eyes darkened and the muscles in his face drew taut. "If our marriage were real," she added, "I wouldn't mind waitin' a year before startin' a family so that we could have time to experiment."

"Experiment."

"You know. Make love whenever, wherever, the mood strikes. Once kids are around, we'd have to be more circumspect. For instance, you wouldn't be able to wear those sweatpants around me without underwear ever again."

He crossed his arms. "Why not?"

She laid a hand high on his thigh. "'Cause it turns me on somethin' fierce, honey. Kinda like what it does to you when I wear a T-shirt and no bra."

"Or *my* shirt with nothing underneath."

She let her hand drift to the inside of his thigh. His response more than gratified her. "Does it turn you on somethin' fierce, Diego?"

"You know it does—" he clamped a hand on hers "—or else you wouldn't be wearing it."

"Misty took away my nightgown and robe. The only other nightgowns I have were gifts from her. You can imagine—"

"Vividly." He moved her hand away. "And on that note, let's go to bed."

"My thoughts exactly."

"You know what I mean."

She smiled lazily. "It was just gettin' interestin', honey."

"You've got a good imagination, Magnolia. Finish it in your dreams." He stood, pulling her up, as well. "Give it whatever conclusion you want."

"I'll do that. How about a little inspiration to take with me?"

He smiled lazily back. "It's pretty much attached to me, *novia*. And not so little, in case you hadn't noticed."

"You'll do," she purred.

"Stop with the flattery, please. You'll swell my head."

She slipped her arms around his back and rubbed her cheek against his chest. "You have willpower, I'll grant you that."

"It has limits."

"But don't test them, right?" She leaned back a little. "The little inspiration I was looking for was a good-night kiss."

With an expression that showed clearly he was just humoring her, he leaned close.

"And not a little peck, either," she said. "Something to dream on."

"Amending rules again, Magnolia?"

"Did we have a rule against good-night kisses? I don't recall your saying anything about it."

He smiled. "You kiss me, then. Show me what you expect."

"My pleasure." She pulled herself toward him, her gaze locked with his, until she found the intimate alignment she wanted between their bodies. "You need to help a little," she whispered.

His expression fierce, he cupped her rear with both hands and held her to him. Their mouths connected a few desire-filled moments later. He tasted as tempting as hot caramel on ice cream, and she hungered for sweet satisfaction. His tongue toyed with hers languidly, then with the tempo of a mating dance. He pulled back. She sighed dreamily.

"So, fifteen seconds qualifies as long enough?" he asked, releasing her.

Her eyes flew open. "You counted?"

"More than a peck, but how long exactly? I had to know your expectations."

"You couldn't just get lost in the moment and not care how long it took?"

He seemed to think about it. "I can be fully involved and still be paying attention. For example, even though I was as aroused as you last night, I also took note of the fact you have a tiny freckle just below and to the left of your navel, and another along the faded tan line of your right buttock. There are other details I could relate, but they would sound crude to you."

J.D. turned out the lights, needing to end the evening, finding his willpower sorely strained and the reasons they shouldn't make love diminishing in importance. Except that she would interpret his giving in as having some sort of significance where their relationship was concerned—and he still couldn't offer her permanence, not until she knew what she was committing to. And now that he knew how much a stable home life meant to her...well, could he ever offer her that?

"The honeymoon is definitely over," she grumbled as she walked away.

"I run every morning," he said as she flipped the switch inside her bedroom door, spilling a shaft of light into the living room. "I'll be back around nine."

"I'll have breakfast ready."

"You don't have to"

"I *want* to. Don't argue with me about it. At least let me pay you back in a way that I can. Good night, Diego." She shut the door with a quiet click.

He laid his hand on the door. "Sweet dreams," he whispered.

Nine

J.D. slowed almost to a walk for the last two blocks of his run at nine o'clock the next morning. Fog layered the air, a quilt of gray mist that dampened everything, saturating his sweaty running clothes to the point of dripping. He swiped at his forehead with the back of his arm. His mind felt clearer now, his purpose unclouded by the tempting lure of uninterrupted contact with Magnolia—her fragrance, her teasing laugh, her seductive smile. And yet contentment washed over him, as well, like a warm bath on a cold winter night. Their relationship changed hourly, it seemed, as their situation forced them closer. Push, pull, push, pull. The one with the most patience wins? A month ago he would have declared himself the patient one without hesitation. But now? Now he could see that she stored a well of patience herself. It was just manifested differently, mostly in unrelenting determination. Heaven help him if she'd made him a goal.

The apartment smelled of coffee and—he sniffed the air—blueberries. He leaned against the door after he shut it, closed his eyes and breathed the homey smells. He could get used to this.

He heard her humming and went in search of her, finding her bent over peering into the oven. When she stood and turned, a smile lit up her face.

"Good morning," she said. "I hope you're hungry. I've made muffins, and everything's ready to go for omelets."

"I usually only eat…"

Maggie raised her brows and crossed her arms.

"Fine," he said. "Great. Let me shower first."

"Take your time. I, um, kind of like your grunge look, though." She was as surprised at her words as he looked. She'd thought a sweaty, glistening man was a temptation only to fictional heroines. She'd been dead wrong. Or maybe it was just *this* sweaty, glistening man whose long, muscular legs were revealed enticingly by the running shorts he wore, and whose flat, solid abdomen was bare to her gaze between the waistband of his shorts and his hacked-off T-shirt. He looked fierce and dark and tempting with his unshaven face and intense brown eyes.

"You like my grunge look?" He leered at her, drawing closer, pulling her into his embrace and smashing her face against his chest with a teasing growl. "Even the smell, Magnolia?"

She sniffed daintily and tipped her head back, intending to wrinkle her nose at him. But it wouldn't have been the truth. He turned her on. Period. Sweat and all.

She leaned away from him a little and slid her hands under his cutoff T-shirt, pushing the garment up to nuzzle the damp, cool skin as he sucked in a breath. She tasted the salt on his skin, wallowed in the masculine scent of him that rose hot and steamy as she caressed him with her mouth and hands, sending his body temperature soaring.

He groaned her name, diving his fingers into her hair as she trailed her tongue down his abdomen. "Don't," he said hoarsely, then more quietly, "Please."

Maggie watched him walk away. When she heard the

shower running, she poured orange juice into crystal stemware. By the time he came into the kitchen, she was tipping his omelet onto a plate.

"You'll spoil me," he said quietly.

"I like to cook. I hope you like to eat."

He relaxed visibly as she handed him the plate. She picked up a pot holder and took her own plate from the oven, along with the muffins.

"It's been a long time since I've had homemade food on any regular basis," he said as they sat at the table.

"And I haven't had company for quite a while, either. Jazz used to come for Sunday supper before she and Patrick got married. Then I started going to their house instead. I miss it—the planning, the shopping, the cooking, setting a nice table."

"That's important to you? Having friends over?"

She nodded. "I'm looking forward to being done with college so I have time to spare."

"Your plans, your dreams," he said hesitantly.

"What about them?"

"What do you see in your future?"

"Well, you already know I'm building a career at home. Even if the writing doesn't work out, the designing I've been doing for Misty could be lucrative. Beyond that, I guess I want what most people want. A house with a yard, a dog and a cat, some kids—the number to be determined later—and a husband who wants the same things out of life that I do."

He looked at her over the rim of his mug. "I have to admit, you've surprised me with your old-fashioned goals."

"I don't think wanting marriage and children is an odd notion."

"Don't get defensive. All I knew of you was what I learned from working beside you, and *that* Magnolia is very different from the one I've come to know in the past month. Tell me how many women of your acquaintance sew and quilt and do all those other things you do."

"I've supported myself for twelve years, so I've had to

budget carefully. Necessity drove me to learn those skills, but passion for it keeps me going.''

"It's time-consuming.''

"So is anything worthwhile.'' She broke a muffin in two. The steam rose, fragrant with blueberries. "I'm a homebody. I'm not going to apologize for it.''

Every time thoughts of a permanent relationship with her intruded, he was reminded of how unsuited they were for each other. If he wanted to advance within his field, he'd have to move, maybe several times over the course of his career. He'd just get settled probably, only to be relocated. He couldn't imagine a worse scenario for a homebody, for someone who had moved constantly as a child and wished for something different.

They finished eating and took care of the dishes. Maggie decided he was brooding about something and that she needed to be quiet and let him. She smiled. It almost made her feel like a real wife, anticipating his moods and adapting to them. She wondered if he'd done the same with her yet.

"Ready to go see your new nephew?'' he asked as he dried the last pan.

"Definitely.''

"I've got a few things to take care of, so I'll drop you off.''

"Aren't you coming in?''

"When I'm done.''

"Oh.'' Another clue the honeymoon was over. She ran her hands through her hair, then picked up her purse and took her coat from the closet. "I imagine Patrick will be glad to see you. I wonder how it feels, becoming a father again at his age.''

"You make forty-seven seem like seventy-four, Magnolia. He's not on his deathbed. He'll be able to toss a football with his son for a while yet.''

"Did you miss that with your father?''

"I missed everything with my father. You know that.'' He punched in the alarm code and shut the door behind them.

"I thought you had a relationship with him now.''

"I do."

"Yet you didn't invite him to the wedding."

"I did invite him."

She waited but he didn't say more. "Will I get to meet him sometime?"

"Probably."

As they drove through the city, Maggie considered his childhood, of which she had only minimal knowledge. Would he share the details if she asked? She analyzed the expression on his face. He was concentrating on driving, his gaze shifting to the rearview mirror a lot, as well as seeming to look at everything as they went along.

"Tell me about your childhood," she said. "Do you still hate your mother?"

He hesitated a few seconds. "Part of me will never forgive her."

"For kidnapping you?"

"Don't use that word. That wasn't what happened."

"But you were taken away from your father and raised in a foreign country."

"Mexico is my mother's birth country. It wasn't foreign to her. She was just…weak. Too weak to fight her family."

"Tell me what did happen."

He tapped his fingers against the steering wheel, and she thought he wasn't going to open up, but he did finally.

"My mother was on vacation here when she was eighteen. She met my father, who was twenty-three and a law student. They fell in love and were married, against the wishes of her family. Maybe they would have had a chance if her family had left her alone, but her father was a powerful man in Mexico and my father was naive. He didn't know the extent of my grandfather's resources, so he didn't expect what happened."

"Your grandfather kidnapped both you and your mother?"

"It wasn't like that, Magnolia. We went on a long visit when my parents thought that her family had finally accepted their marriage. My father was practicing law by then but he was just building his career, so he let us go without him. He was to come for the last week of our visit. I was not quite three years old. When he arrived, her father told him that she wouldn't be returning, that there would be a divorce."

"Your mother didn't even see him? She didn't fight it?"

"She was a dutiful daughter who had been brainwashed to believe my father was the enemy and that her place was with her family. My father used every means available to speak with her, and to get me back. But we'd been sent away, then kept away long enough for me to forget anything about my father."

She laid a hand on his arm. "How awful for you."

He curved a hand over hers, holding it there a moment, seeming to need her touch. "Worse for my father. He was told we died in an auto accident a year or so after their divorce was final. He didn't know what to believe, but when you're as powerful as my grandfather, you can make anything happen. He supposedly proved our deaths. My father had to accept it."

"How did you learn all this?"

"Eventually the guilt was too much for my mother. She had remarried—a man of her father's choosing—and had given birth to two children. After she told me about my father I became obsessed with wanting to meet him. I was fourteen and rebellious. I came to resent the restrictions on my life, put there by my grandfather."

"Did you like your stepfather?"

"He was kind to me, but I wasn't his. Ana and Lorenzo, my sister and brother, were his true children. I always felt the difference. And my grandfather made it clear that Lorenzo would be heir to his business because his father was not American."

They parked in front of Jasmine and Patrick's house and continued the conversation.

"When I was seventeen I made my way out of the country and showed up unannounced on my father's doorstep, knowing only enough English to get me to his house."

"How did your father react?"

Diego's hands tightened around the steering wheel. He looked through the windshield, remembering. "He cried, and laughed. Hugged me until I couldn't breathe. He knew Spanish, of course. He'd learned some from my mother and then had become fluent when he searched for us. He kept saying that he knew I hadn't died. He knew it."

"How did you feel?"

"Scared. Happy. Free for the first time." He loosened his grip on the steering wheel. "And very sad for my mother. My father's a good man. He would have given her a fine life if she'd let him. After the initial euphoria, I went through an angry period, angry that he hadn't searched harder. I thought he never should have given up, I suppose. It wasn't until some years had passed that I forgave him, not until I really understood how little the government can do to help find stolen children, particularly when a legal guardian has taken the child."

"Have you seen your mother since you left?"

"Once. When my grandfather died. My mother and I were like strangers. Too much had happened. I call her occasionally, and I do talk to Ana and Lorenzo at least once a month. Ana is married and has a baby of her own."

Maggie brushed his hair with her fingers, needing to touch him. "I had no idea your life had been so...challenging. You didn't have a normal childhood, either."

"For me, life was just confusing. Sometimes conversation would stop when I entered a room. My mother suffered from depressions that would last for days."

"How did it change you? What difference did it make on your life?" she asked.

"I believe in rules more, I think, so there is less chaos. I believe children should not ever be pawns for their parents' purposes. I believe marriage is forever, unless there is abuse, physical or mental."

"So do I," she said softly.

He searched her face with his gaze. "Ours isn't a real marriage, Magnolia. We had no choice."

"I chose."

He closed his eyes. "No. No, don't think that way. I was afraid of this." He blew out a breath. She didn't know him. She didn't know what he did. She hadn't made an informed decision to marry him. "We are attracted to each other. Proximity isn't helping."

"You can think that all you like, if it helps you get through the days. It isn't the way I feel."

"It isn't real," he repeated.

She just smiled.

He cupped the back of her neck and slid a finger along the edge of her sweater, needing to be sure she was wearing the necklace. He felt her arch toward him, but he just massaged her neck and shoulders as they sat in silence a little while. Finally, he pulled his hand away. He glanced at her purse. "Do you have your pager?"

"I think so." She opened the bag and hunted until she found it.

"Turn it on, please."

"If you need me, you can just call—"

"Humor me, Magnolia."

J.D. shook his head as he stared at the schedule posted inside Maggie's kitchen cabinet. He'd never known anyone to list their household chores by day. Today was Tuesday—ironing day. She hadn't done any. Would it throw her off schedule for the whole week? He was glad she'd decided to take a nap instead after visiting her sister.

He shut the cabinet door and looked around the kitchen at the sparkling window and polished sink, at the orderly counters and delicate curtains. The written schedule, she'd told him, reduced stress. She didn't have to think about what needed to be done because she already knew. She didn't have to find time to clean because it was part of her routine, along with school and work.

"But everything is spotless," he'd said.

"Of course it is. Because I keep it that way. Nobody notices a *clean* toilet."

He smiled at the memory of her pointing that fact out to him, then he glanced at the clock. Time to wake her up if they were going to eat before work.

He opened her bedroom door quietly. The late-afternoon sun striped the bed with light and shadow from her window blinds. Her clothes were folded across a chair back, her lacy robin's egg blue bra and matching panties draped over the top. His imagination peeled back the bedcovers and looked at her, curled on her side, her hands tucked under her cheek. Memories of her body lit his mind. Slender and pale and surprisingly curvy—she'd been more than he'd imagined.

He eased close to the bed and was hypnotized by her bare shoulder peeking above the edge of the comforter. Tempted beyond thought, he knelt and pressed his lips to the warm, smooth skin. She stirred, then resettled.

"Magnolia?"

"Hmm?"

"It's time to wake up."

"Okay." She didn't move.

"Are you awake?"

"Mmm-hmm."

He smiled. "Your eyes are closed."

"I don't want you to go away." She opened her eyes and rolled onto her back, then withdrew her arm from under the covers and stroked his face, resting her thumb against his lips until his eyes darkened.

"You kissed me on the shoulder. Your version of Prince Charming waking Sleeping Beauty?"

He shrugged, then stood and walked to the door. "Don't read too much into it," he cautioned before he left the room.

Maggie bounded out of bed as soon as he shut the door. Stretching luxuriously, she smiled, happy that she'd caught him in an unguarded moment of temptation. She liked being irresistible. A couple of sharp knocks sounded on her bedroom door before it swung open.

"Can I do anything to start din—"

They froze in unison.

"I'm sorry. I didn't expect—" he swallowed visibly "—you to be out of bed so fast."

She lowered her arms and faced him fully, lightly shaking her hair back, thrilled at his open admiration. "Want to help me get dressed?" she asked with a grin. He took a step back, so she turned away to pick up her lacy panties. When she turned around, he was there, inches from her, waiting.

He extended a hand. In slow motion, she passed him the garment.

The sunlight and shadow streaking into the room gave the moment the texture and artistry of a Van Gogh painting as he bent on one knee and held the silky bit of nothing for her to step into. She placed a hand on his head to balance herself as he rested his cheek against her abdomen, his hair feathering her skin, his breath dusting her lightly, drawing a shiver from her.

He slid the garment up and over her hips, then he stood and reached for her bra.

She slipped her arms under the straps. "Your willpower is beyond human. But in proving it, you make me ache."

He settled the cups over her breasts before he fastened the front clasp. Then he looked into her eyes. "I can take care of the ache for you, Magnolia. It wouldn't take but a minute."

"Bragger."

He smiled. "It wasn't a commentary on my skill but on your own passion."

"Your offer is tempting." She looped her arms around his neck and pulled herself snugly to him. "But I decided that there will be no climaxes for either of us until we can do so together."

He cupped her rear, holding her still. "We could climax right here and right now, simultaneously. It would still take but a minute."

"I'll wait."

At her pleasantly determined tone of voice, he released her. He watched as she swept up her jeans and pulled them on, then scooped up her sweatshirt and tugged it over her head. She picked up her shoes and socks and sat on the edge of the bed.

She gave him a slow once-over look. "And if I have to wait until we're no longer married to make love with you, I can do that, too, honey."

The *so, there!* tone reverberated in the room until the absurdity of her words drew a chuckle from him.

"You can quit laughing now," she called as he left her room. "I didn't marry you to be your entertainment."

"Too late," he called back.

Ten

The last hill of J.D.'s morning run was the killer. He welcomed it. Almost two weeks of sharing space with Maggie had given him a short fuse. Running helped as tension the likes of which he'd never known dogged his steps and destroyed his sleep.

And Magnolia was the cause of it all.

She cooked his meals and ironed his shirts. He made beds and vacuumed. She cleaned and polished. He washed dishes. She dried, talking all the while, making him share stories.

Piece by tempting piece, he watched her create a pale pink negligee for Misty's new line, adding a new section daily to the garment draped on the dressmaker's form in his room, leaving behind snippets of lace and lingering perfume he could smell when he woke during the night.

She'd stopped teasing him. He had nothing to complain about. That she was waiting for him to make the next move was staggeringly clear.

His need for her intensified with every unintentional sway

of her hips, every cheerful "Good morning," every quiet turning of a page as she studied.

He resented how happy she seemed to be. And he wished like hell that Hastings would take the bait so neatly offered him.

J.D. crested the hill and slowed to a walk. He was half a block away from the apartment when he spotted a black limousine parked in front of her apartment. The tinted window of the passenger door glided down as he approached. He bent to peer inside, starkly aware that he was without his gun.

"Join me for a minute."

Hastings could make a command seem like a party invitation, J.D. thought, crouching by the door instead. "I'd drip sweat all over your fancy upholstery."

"Get in."

He opened the door and slid in, unobtrusively activating the recorder in his pager as he settled in the seat. Hastings passed him a small towel, holding it fastidiously between his thumb and forefinger. J.D. pressed his face in it, then rubbed his hair leisurely, eyeing the man who was dressed impeccably, his own hair styled and sprayed.

Hastings leaned back and crossed one leg over the other, fussing with his trouser crease. "I never asked you—how was your honeymoon?"

"Too short."

"Why didn't you take some time? Go somewhere exotic?"

"You know the answer to that."

"Ah, yes." Hastings pulled out a flat, gold case from inside his suit jacket, extracted a cigarette and lit it. He enjoyed a few drags before he spoke again. "You're waiting for me to decide."

J.D. nodded.

"Your terms are generous. And my current...supplier has gotten greedy. But something niggles at me about you."

J.D. grabbed the door handle and pulled. "You've danced one too many two-steps for me. Get yourself another partner."

"Step out of this car and you're dead."

He paused. He'd dealt with a lot of lowlifes. None of them set him on edge like this educated, intelligent, sophisticated man. At least the scumbags had been predictable. "What's the problem, Mr. Hastings? I come highly recommended—you told me so yourself. Your money comes out as clean as an April shower. No cops are sniffing my trail. I've facilitated transfers amounting to millions."

"Something about you just doesn't ring true, Duran. I've checked you out but it's nothing I can put my finger on."

"It's reasonable that we don't trust each other." He angled toward Hastings. "I'll be honest. Your business would improve my standard of living. But if we're not going to deal, say so now. I've turned down other clients because you've arranged to meet me, then never showed. I'm a businessman, same as you."

"Not quite the same."

"Everyone starts somewhere."

Hastings ground out his cigarette. "I'll be in touch."

"I'll give you one more chance. You know where to find me."

"We'll deal when I say so, Duran. Do tell that little spitfire you married to be careful. Wouldn't want to see you a widower so soon after being a groom."

Everything inside him seized up. "Is that a threat?"

"You can't be too cautious these days, can you? Accidents happen. Brakes fail. Drive-by shootings are becoming commonplace. Distressing, isn't it? What is the world coming to? Enjoy her, Duran."

Before it's too late. J.D. filled in the rest as he climbed out of the limo and shut the door, careful not to slam it or show any emotion at all.

He called his boss to relate the event, was advised to get Maggie out of town, then was threatened again with reassignment.

"You're way too personally involved here," Callahan said. "If you pull me out, you'll never get Hastings. I want to tell the parents of those two women that we found their killer, don't you?''

"Not at the expense of your wife's life, or yours."

"Her car broke down yesterday. I'll make sure it isn't fixed soon so that I have to take her everywhere. Novacek already watches her when I can't—which is rare enough. She'll be all right. I can tell you now that she would never agree to leave town. Not without concrete facts."

"Maybe you should tell her."

"You don't know her. She'd want to be involved. She'd want to help catch him. She isn't trained for this, Cal. I can't take that risk."

Callahan's sigh made J.D. wonder at his chances for career advancement. "Okay. We play it your way for now. Let's talk tomorrow morning about some extra security."

"Great. Thanks."

After sitting for a few minutes mapping a strategy, he stripped off his running clothes and climbed into the shower, yanking the curtain shut. Hastings needed to dominate and control. J.D. had been letting him. They only butted heads about Magnolia, and that was because Hastings knew she was his hot button. Hastings expected a reaction, so J.D. had to give him one.

He ducked his head under the spray, then squirted some shampoo into his palm. When he was done lathering, he soaped his body and rinsed off, then stayed under the spray, letting the hot water loosen his muscles. He had half an hour before he'd have to leave to pick up Magnolia from school, time enough to make the beds and—

He tensed as the high-pitched wail of the security alarm penetrated the noise of the shower. He waited, and counted. After more than twelve seconds it stopped. Too long. About eight seconds too long. About the length of time it would take for someone unfamiliar with the code to shut down the system.

Leaving the water running, he stepped out of the shower and picked up his gun from the vanity. Three doors accessed the bathroom, one from the living room, one from each bedroom. All were closed. Water dripped down his face. He shifted his gaze from door to door, watching the handles as he took shallow breaths. The living room doorknob turned. He inched toward it.

The door eased open. Gun in hand, he grabbed the knob and jerked. "Freeze!"

Maggie froze. A scream locked in her throat. She stared straight down the barrel of a gun, behind which a dripping and naked J.D. loomed.

"*Madre de Dios,* Magnolia!" He pointed the gun toward the floor and took his finger off the trigger. "What are you doing home?"

"I—I called. My last class was canceled." She swallowed. "I left you a mess—"

"I could have killed you," he said, the words hoarse and desperate. "I could have killed you."

On some level she noted the horror in his voice—the fear, the relief, the frustration. Then sight overruled every other sense. She took a hypnotic step forward, taking in the beauty of his body, the sculpted muscles, the lean, tapering form and pure masculinity. *Ask him about the gun. Why does he have—* "You're so beautiful," she said instead, unable to let logic surface. "You're so incredibly—"

He hauled her to him, kissed her with the passion of a man who'd just found salvation. Maggie wrapped her arms around him, opened her mouth to his nipping teeth and exploring tongue, moaned her acceptance of the invasion. She winced as his fingers dove into her hair and tipped her head back farther. His eyes glittered like obsidian, hard and shiny, before he attacked her mouth again. He dragged her impossibly closer, enveloping her in his arms as he tucked her under his chin, his arms a vise from which she couldn't escape, his breathing harsh and deep.

She ran tentative hands down his sides.

"No more," he said harshly. "No more waiting."

He whipped her sweater over her head, peeled off her

T-shirt, tore away her bra, all the while moving her toward her bedroom, a trail of clothes in their wake, his hands sailing along her body as more skin was revealed, teasing her with a tenderness that made the fast and furious removal of her clothes even more erotic. Kneeling, he yanked off her shoes, tugged her jeans down, stripped away her panties, along with her jeans and socks. He pressed his face to her abdomen and breathed deeply. Overwhelmed by how he cherished her, she went weak. When he stood again, she saw unguarded hunger in the taut muscles of his face and the set of his mouth.

She said nothing, afraid that if she did, the moment would shatter like so many before that had teased her with consummation and discovery. She rested her hands on his chest and slid them lower until she could capture his rigid masculine heat in her hands. His eyes closed to slits. His head fell back. The room echoed with his deep moan of pained need. He let her explore him, although not nearly long enough. Then he cupped her head again and tipped it back. When his mouth came down hard on hers, she knew she'd come home.

"Now," she whispered when he slanted their mouths differently. "Oh, I need you, Diego. I need you so much."

His expression was fierce, yet his hands wondrously gentle as they stroked her flesh, feathering her throat, curving around and under her breasts to lift them high as he watched, then gliding along her abdomen and beyond, teasing with fingertips soft as velvet. He eased her backward until she came up against the side of the bed. Reaching behind her he sent the bedcovers sailing and laid her on the cool sheet, blanketing her with his body, sliding his hands under her to shift her up farther, then settling against her.

He groaned as their bodies touched, arched up as if the contact alone would send him over the edge.

He whispered her name and tears welled in her eyes at the gentleness and wonder and power that rang in the one word. Before she could wrap her legs around him, he slid down her, scraping his unshaven jaw against her, trailing his open mouth along her skin, drawing tiny bumps of reaction. When he took a pebbled nipple deep in his mouth and suckled her, she curved her arms over his head, holding him there, arching higher to beg without words for more, much more. He tasted the other tight crest, lapped at her, bit lightly, suckled harder, whispered words in a language she couldn't understand. Only the tone was universal. He rose above her, almost a stranger to her as the hard edge of passion consumed him and transferred to her.

His gaze never wavering from hers, he slid a hand to her knee and pulled her leg over his hip, holding her still. She closed her eyes as the hot, slick tip of him found its warm welcome.

"*Mírame,* Magnolia." The lyrical words filled her soul with music. "Look at me."

She forced her eyes open and he filled her, fully, beautifully, perfectly, the power and strength of him lighting a fire that flared hot and fast, burning toward an explosion that expanded with the fuel of motion and sound and wishes granted. The power of it shocked her, and because he was watching her so closely, he saw.

"It's all right."

His voice wasn't soothing, but strained, as if convincing himself as well, inciting her further. A fireball coiled and sizzled deep within her.

"Let it happen, *novia.*"

"Diego…"

"I know."

And even though her eyes were open, she was blind to everything, the heat and intensity shimmering so white that she couldn't even see him, only knew when he was consumed by the same inferno.

J.D. felt her whole body soften beneath him. He didn't want to look at her, didn't want to see her expression in the aftermath, now stark with sunlight that illuminated the room, lighting truths and deceits. He had to say something to her. He had no idea what.

Regret battled contentment. He'd never broken his word before. And because he hadn't been able to control his need, he'd set her up to be hurt even further, to have her hate him now instead of later. All the happiness he'd seen grow in her was destined to die.

When she fidgeted he rolled to his side, bringing her with him, tucking her close so that she couldn't look at him. He swept a hand down her back, tracing the smooth, silky curves, finally resting on the taut, damp flesh of her rear.

"Cold?" he asked.

She nuzzled his chest and forced a leg between his. "No way."

He could swear she purred.

Instinct told him she wouldn't respond well to an apology from him. The moment had been unplanned and uncontrollable, but it had happened. Any attempt at excusing it would be cowardly and cruel.

"That was amazing," she said on a sigh, drawing tiny circles on his stomach with her fingernails, inching lower.

He sucked in a breath. "Yes."

She angled her shoulder and pushed against him so that he rolled onto his back. In a fluid movement she straddled his thighs.

She tucked her hair behind her ears, revealing a face that was softly flushed and shimmering with fresh confidence. She was naked, except for his necklace. *Dios.* Now what? She expected more from him. More would be a conscious choice. More would be unforgivable.

More would be paradise.

"We're so different," she said, stroking him as his need for her grew at her curious touch.

He reached for her.

"Not yet," she said. "I love to watch your body change like this. Everything gets harder. Your thighs, your stomach, your hands, even your jaw. Your whole body gets aroused, doesn't it? I didn't realize."

Ah, Magnolia, how innocent you are. How temptingly open.

How beautifully made. "Do you think you stay soft, *novia?* You're the same."

"Am I?"

Placing a hand on each shoulder, he pulled her toward him, until he could take a taut nipple in his mouth. "Hard now. Even harder in a minute," he said, proving his point as he drew a soft moan from her. He opened his mouth to hers as she shifted to kiss him with a purity of intention that was frightening. Everything was so simple to her.

She rose slightly to let him position himself beneath her, then she released a long sound of pleasure as she sank onto him.

"You fill me so tightly, so completely," she said, her hands pressing the sides of his head, her thumbs tracing his cheekbones. "We were made for each other."

He didn't know what to say to her, so he helped her sit up and use her thigh muscles to ride him, gently at first, then faster and more powerfully. He pressed a thumb to the hot core of her and stroked the tiny nub lightly.

"You get hard here, as well, *novia.*"

She arched back, stretching her arms behind her to rest her hands on his thighs. With his eyes he followed the sway of her breasts, the lift of her pelvis, the fascinating motion of her thigh muscles contracting, relaxing, contracting, relaxing. He brought his other hand into play and sent her over the top, relishing the sounds that filtered from her. Then just as she relaxed forward, he rolled her over and pushed home, hard and rhythmically and relentlessly, taking her up again. He swallowed her words with his demanding mouth, their tongues mating as slickly as their bodies, their driving rhythm creating a force so powerful, they almost generated sparks.

"Diego," she moaned as the full impact carried her to the edge and held her there. She clawed him and he welcomed the pressure.

"Magnolia," he groaned back, poised on the same brink but waiting.

A few more thrusts, a few more arching lifts, then flight. Finally, a soft landing and sleep.

The jangle of the telephone sliced into his dream. No, it wasn't a dream, after all. She was there with him. He felt her reach across him, pick up the phone and say hello.

"Just a minute, please." She passed him the phone.

"Hello?"

"It's Novacek. Since she answered the phone, I assume everything's all right."

J.D. glanced her way. "Yes. What happened?"

"I followed her to class, then went to get some coffee. I was there when class was supposed to be dismissed. She was already gone."

"Where are you?"

"Across the street."

"I want to talk with you."

"I've got to get over to the Misty Nights Lingerie warehouse."

He watched Magnolia sit up beside him, enjoyed the beauty of the pale, slender back revealed to the tempting curve of her bottom. "Uh…" He could hardly think. "Uh, why?"

"Didn't you hear? Somebody trashed the place."

"*What?*" He sat straight up. "When?"

"During the night."

"I'm going over there." He looked at Magnolia as she turned to face him. The quilt had pulled away when he moved. He swallowed. "I need you to stay where you are," he said into the phone.

Content, Maggie watched him watch her. Everything had changed. Her life had veered down a whole new path. She was different because of loving him. And different from having shared the deepest intimacy possible between a man and woman. He had to feel it, too.

She smiled and reached for him as he hung up the phone.

"Misty's warehouse was trashed." He threw the covers aside. "I need to see how she is doing."

"Me, too." The mood shattered, she had thoughts now only for her friend.

He stopped her with a hand on her shoulder as she followed the trail of her clothing. "I don't think that's a good idea."

She straightened, her panties in one hand, jeans in the other. His eyes didn't stray from hers. "Why not?"

"Too many people—"

"What are you, the invisible man? If you can go, I can go." What was going on? She thought they'd just reached accord in their marriage and here he was, being Mr. Macho again. "Misty's my friend. I want to help."

He turned from her. She watched him pull open a dresser drawer, remove gray cotton briefs and step into them.

"You're right, of course," he said.

She dressed as he did, almost garment for garment, so that they were ready at the same time. "I don't understand how you and Misty got to be so close," she said tentatively as they went out the front door and down the stairs.

"She's easy to know. Easy to like."

"Oh, she's one of the most down-to-earth people I know. But what's her connection with you?"

J.D. sent a hand signal Novacek's way as she climbed into the car. He settled behind the wheel. "There aren't many people I call friend, Magnolia, but Misty's one of them."

"What about me?"

He waited until they reached a red light, then he turned toward her. Her eyes were full of anticipation. What could he say to her? Friendship was the least of what he felt. And after the lovemaking—

"What about me?" she repeated even more softly.

He traced her face with his fingertips, not speaking. A car honked, alerting him that the light had turned green. He used it as an excuse not to answer.

Thirty percent of Misty's spring line had been destroyed before the police could respond to the silent alarm. J.D. knew, as did Misty, that it was retribution for her interfering on New Year's Eve.

"My insurance will cover the losses," Misty said as they huddled in the manager's office, both of them watching Maggie through a plate-glass window as she peered in box after box, staring at the garments drenched in black dye. "But the delays in getting the goods to the stores will be devastating. If I can't fill the orders, the results will show up next season in reduced orders. A smart businessman like Brendan understands that."

"We'll get him, Misty. I promise you."

"Duncan said the same thing. Still, it hurts. I've worked for so long to get to this point. I was just getting comfortable enough to take some time off." She sighed. "Well, back to the sewing machines. Thanks for checking on me."

"I'm glad the judge was with you."

"It was kind of nice sharing the burden." She smiled as Maggie looked up and made a sad face their way. "Have you told her about Brendan yet?"

"Only a little."

"What are you waiting for?"

"The right time."

She patted his arm. "One thing I've learned, J.D. The right time doesn't ever come on its own. The right time is always a choice you make."

J.D. thought about Misty's words as he dropped Magnolia off at home, much against her wishes. He knew there was unfinished business between them. He knew he was stalling. He was tired of fighting his feelings, especially after this morning. But he knew he had to continue to do so.

"I'm in a hell of a mess," J.D. said as he grabbed the window frame in his father's den and stared at the foliage outside. "How did this happen? I thought I had everything under control."

"You're human, Jimmy."

He turned and crossed his arms. "That's it? That's all the

fatherly advice I get? I didn't use protection, Dad. What happens if… *Dios.* I can't believe it didn't even occur to me."

"Maybe she's on the Pill."

"If she is, she doesn't keep them in the bathroom or beside her bed. What she does keep in the table beside *my* bed, as I discovered the first night, are a couple of condoms. That should tell you something."

"Since I sincerely doubt she left them there in case you brought another woman home," his father said, humor lacing his words, "it tells me she's prepared."

"It tells *me* it's her method of birth control." J.D. ran his hands through his hair. "If she's pregnant, I won't let her go. I will be a father to that child."

"Is pregnancy your only fear, son?"

"Of course. What else?"

His father leveled a look at him. "Life works out as it's supposed to. I finally learned that. I hope you will learn from my experience, son, and accept what you cannot change. Perhaps this is a sign you should tell her the truth."

"If I tell her the truth, she'll start looking over her shoulder," J.D. said, exasperated. "She'll clue Hastings into her feelings the first time she sees him, even though she would believe she's hiding it well. If I tell her the truth, she'll fear him a hundred times more than she does now. He'll know it, and he'll prey on it. My only chance to keep her safe is to keep her ignorant."

"I think you don't give her enough credit, Jimmy." He held up a hand. "I also admit you know her well and I don't. But perhaps you should force her to leave town."

"*He has threatened to kill her.* Because of me, her life is in danger, and I can't show any fear. *Neither can she.* We're so close now to nailing him. So close. If I have her hidden away, he'd take that as weakness on my part. I'd be dead."

"Damned if you do. Damned if you don't."

"And whatever the consequences, I'll have to live with them. Still, I know in my heart she's safer with me."

* * *

Maggie couldn't wait to get home. She breezed through the night at work, anxious to be alone with her husband.

Her husband. Finally she could say the words honestly. She turned toward him as he pulled into the garage, traced his profile with her eyes, wondered at his silence. She smiled as she pictured the evening ahead. She would wear the red teddy Misty had given her for her birthday and the spicy perfume he'd commented on twice.

Candles waited to be lit; chilled champagne waited to be savored.

This would be their wedding night. Tonight she would tell him she loved him.

His hand rested at the small of her back as they climbed the stairs. Anticipation simmered in her, warm, gentle bubbles of expectation. The rightness of what they'd shared made her sigh.

"Tired?" he asked as he shut the door and entered the security code.

"No." She turned and smiled. "In fact, I think I'll take a quick shower. Care to join me?"

J.D. walked past her. The hopeful look in her eyes stoked the fire of guilt already burning his stomach. He dreaded seeing that brilliant light of happiness dim inside her.

He looked at the answering machine. No messages.

"Diego?"

Face her. Don't be a coward. He turned around. "What?"

"What's wrong?"

He stared at her a minute longer. "Let's sit down."

She blinked, surprised. Hesitance rang in her voice. "I don't think I want to. Just tell me."

"What happened today? Why did you come home so early?"

"My last class was canceled and a friend offered to drop me off. I called before I left campus so that you wouldn't bother coming."

"I was preoccupied this morning. I guess I forgot to check the machine."

"I knew you'd be home to shower after you ran, so I figured you'd get my message. I also..."

"What?"

She looked away from him, uncomfortable. "There was a man."

"What man? What did he do?"

The ferocity in his voice startled her. She tried to soothe him. "At school for the past couple of days, I've noticed this man hanging around. He hasn't spoken to me, but he's watching. I needed to get away from campus before he caught up with me again. If I'd kept trying your various phone numbers, he might have seen me."

Diego rubbed a hand across his face. She couldn't decipher his expression.

"And don't you dare offer to walk me to class from now on. I've taken self-defense classes. I can protect myself."

"All right, Magnolia."

His acquiescence surprised her. He wasn't reacting the way she expected him to.

"Why did you take so long to turn off the security alarm?" he asked.

"I've rarely had to set it since we got married. I blanked out for a minute. I was just going to open the bathroom door a crack and tell you it was me. I didn't expect— Well, I certainly didn't realize I'd have a gun in my face. Do you have a license for that?"

"A permit. Of course I do." He looked straight at her. "What happened today was a mistake."

She folded her arms across her stomach, warding off his words. "It was beautiful."

"But a mistake nonetheless."

"For you, maybe. Not for me."

He ran his hands through his hair. "I won't excuse it. I was responsible. It was all my fault."

"Damn right it was." She tossed her head, not giving him any quarter. "I'd intentionally kept my distance. I didn't do anything to tease you, or force you."

"I didn't think—"

"That's garbage, Diego. The first time—maybe, *maybe* I could believe that. The tension between us was high. Something set you off. I could grant you the heat-of-the-moment excuse for the first time. But you made love to me a second time. That's calculated. You had plenty of time to think."

"You're right, of course."

She moved in on him. Her eyes shimmered; her mouth quivered. "Now what?"

"Now we go back to where we were."

She made a rude sound.

"I know it's a lot to ask," he said. "I know you don't understand."

"Well, you're right about that. And I'd ask you to explain, except that right now the last thing I want is to hear any lame excuses. So, you want to chalk this one up to experience?" she asked, a haughty lift to her brows. "Okay. Placing blame isn't going to help. And, in truth, I'd have to accept some of the blame because I had expectations that didn't match yours. That's not your fault. But now we've got a bridge between us. Sometime, we're going to have to cross it or burn it."

Maggie swallowed the lump in her throat. Damn him. *Damn* him. She loved him. She loved the stupid rigidity of his stupid decisions. She loved that he was confused and bewildered and unsure. She loved that he couldn't stop himself this afternoon, then was burdened by his conscience. Because he believed in rules to prevent chaos, he'd convinced himself he was doing the right thing.

The ache of rejection pounded in her head. She'd known he wouldn't be an easy man to love. She just wished he wouldn't keep proving her right.

"So," she said with false cheer. "Tomorrow we start anew."

"That's more than generous, Magnolia."

"Yeah, well, I'm a hell of a woman, honey." She started to walk away, then stopped and looked at him. "Why did you come charging out—with a gun? Who were you expecting?"

"I didn't believe it could be you. Anyone else would only be an intruder."

She'd thought *she* was hurting, but deep in his eyes she saw apology and pain, too. The glimpse into his soul comforted her, and gave her hope. *You don't have a clue, James Diego Duran. I'm the best thing that ever happened to you. And I'm not going to go gently out of your life.*

Eleven

"**I** hate being without my car." The statement had become Maggie's mantra for the past week. "What's taking so long for the part to come in?" she asked J.D. as he drove her to class.

"The age of your car, the mechanic said. I already explained that, Magnolia. When it comes in, he'll call us."

"Aren't you getting sick of driving me everywhere?"

"Not at all."

"But you can't even go for your run until you've dropped me at school. Your day gets off to such a late start."

He tossed her a quick glance. "It doesn't bother me."

"Well, it bothers me," she grumbled, slouching in the seat. "I don't see why we can't rent a car until mine's ready."

"Because I'm available to take you."

She blew out a breath. "All this togetherness is..."

"Driving you crazy?" Was she operating under the misconception that it was any easier for him? Memories of their lovemaking haunted and teased him.

She offered him a reluctant smile. "The only time you leave me alone is after you've taken me home from work, when I couldn't possibly go anywhere, anyway. Now, tell me again what it is you're doing at that time of night...or morning, actually."

"I am developing my own business. The man who I'm consulting with works days. I work nights. It's the only time we can meet."

Hastings was finally cooperating. After two more aborted attempts to meet, he'd sent his underlings to do the actual cash transfer. It was a start.

J.D. cast another glance Magnolia's way and saw her drum her fingers on the armrest. He wished he could say something to help her relax.

"Just as long as you're not meeting another woman," she said quietly as they pulled into the school entrance.

The words hit him hard. "What? Late at night? Is that what's got you so worried?"

"Well, it makes sense. There's less contact between us with every passing day. I just figured you had to be—"

"How can you even think it?" He pulled into the drop-off area in front of the campus library and turned off the engine. Of course there was less contact—he couldn't take much more of living with her, being pampered by her, being her husband in fact but not in deed. Despite what she thought, he wasn't superhuman. "I never thought my honor would be in question."

"I didn't mean to offend you," she said, toying with the buckle on her book bag. "I don't know what to think. You seem glad to be chauffeuring me everywhere. Most men would hate it."

"I don't."

She eyed him speculatively. "This has something to do with the gun, doesn't it?"

"I don't know what you mean."

She held up a hand and ticked off items as she spoke. "One, the gun. Two, your fear for my safety. Three, Brendan Hastings. They're all tied together somehow. I just can't figure what your late-night appointments have to do with everything.''

''What makes you think Hastings has anything to do with this?''

''You've never been deferential to him, as an employee should be to a member of the club. And he seems to taunt you somehow, sometimes just with his eyes. He isn't the one who's giving you business advice, is he? Because I wouldn't trust anything he says.''

He angled toward her. ''Hastings is not pleased that I snatched you from under his nose. He's probably denied little in life. We don't like each other. That's a fact. But the reasons are obvious.''

''So, it's just a male territorial thing? Because I understand feeling territorial. All women do.'' She looked out the side window, hiding her face from him.

He cupped her shoulder.

''Don't. Just...don't.'' She twisted out of reach, grabbing the door handle at the same time and opening the door. She hesitated. ''Are you working for Brendan?''

With an oath, J.D. grabbed her arm and spun her toward him. ''Brendan Hastings runs a prostitution ring that stretches from here to his home in Miami. Do you think I would work for someone like that?''

Frustrated, he let go of her to clench the steering wheel and look out the window.

She climbed out of the car, then leaned in to grab her book bag. ''Not by choice.''

She stared at him for a full ten seconds. He stared back.

''I think when you trust someone,'' she said slowly, ''you should trust completely.''

''I think you're going to be late for class.''

He winced as she slammed the door. He'd been a fool to think this could work.

He watched her hurry up the path beside the library, saw Novacek in his latest disguise push himself away from the building and follow her, then he started the engine and headed for home, needing to run, needing to figure out where to go from here.

Brendan Hastings stopped at the maître d's podium on his way out of the Carola that night.

"Is there something you need?" J.D. asked.

"Let's get together tonight."

"All right." J.D. caught Maggie staring at them from the door to the dining room, her brow furrowed. Could she be any more obvious? *Dios.* He should have bitten his tongue.

Although she hadn't been Hastings's server, her revulsion of him had been clear all night—in her posture, in the way her mouth drew into a hard line, in the way she wouldn't make eye contact, even for a second.

"You received verification of your deposit?" J.D. asked as Hastings lingered.

"If I hadn't, you wouldn't be standing here." He turned to leave, then glanced back at J.D. "How much does your wife know about your little side business? If she knows—"

"She does not."

"Really? I'm sensing something different about her. I hope I'm wrong. I don't like loose ends."

"Do not threaten me."

"Or what?"

"I am not without resources of my own, Mr. Hastings." *Damn it, Magnolia. Stay put.* No such luck. She walked to where the men stood. Resigned, J.D. invited her near with a gesture. She slid an arm around his waist and leaned against him as he tugged her closer. Her fingers dug into him, revealing feelings she probably thought she was hiding well.

"Ah, Maggie, my dear. You're looking exceptionally beautiful tonight."

"Marriage agrees with me."

"I can see that. So, am I forgiven for New Year's Eve?"

She placed a palm against J.D.'s abdomen and smiled at him. "Of course. You didn't know."

J.D. almost laughed. She thought she was protecting him in some way. How the tables had turned.

The front door opened and laughter floated in with the cool winter evening. They all turned as Misty Champion breezed in on Judge Shaunnessey's arm. "Behave, Duncan," she said, her eyes sparkling. "Well. Good evening, everyone."

The judge cupped her elbow lightly and led her forward. He looked years younger, Maggie decided, and Misty glowed.

"I met your wife today, Brendan," Misty said. "She's absolutely charming."

The color drained from his face. "My wife is in town?"

"Oh, dear. Did I ruin a surprise? I was sure you'd seen each other by now. Oh, I'm so sorry. Please don't let on to her."

"Wait," he called as they started to turn away. "Where did you see her?"

"We met at Gregorio's, that delightful new avant-garde designer on Maiden Lane. When she told me she hadn't seen you in weeks, we decided she needed something special to wear tonight." She leaned toward him. "I hadn't figured you for a leather-and-chains man, Brendan." She patted the judge's arm. "Of course, I hadn't figured Duncan for one, either. Life is full of surprises, isn't it? Good evening."

Brendan visibly pulled himself together after the couple left. "Well. It seems I'm in for a treat tonight. I guess that means my other plans need to be canceled."

He bid them good-night.

"I had a hard time looking him in the eye, knowing what I know now," Maggie commented as Brendan left. "Can't you do anything about him?"

"Like what?"

"Like report him to the police. Like get him kicked out of here so we don't have to look at him. He makes my skin crawl."

"Believe me, I'm no happier about this than you are."

"Well, I'm going to talk to Judge Shaunnessey about it. There must be something we can do."

"Leave it alone, Magnolia. It's being handled." He couldn't tell her anything else. Hastings had already picked up on something. If she knew more, she'd reveal more. *Dios.* What a mess.

"How do you— Never mind. Don't ask, don't tell, right? I'll tell you one thing. He's afraid of his wife."

J.D. was thinking the same thing. This was information that couldn't wait until morning. "I have to go out tonight."

Maggie moved away from him, knowing she had to get back to work. Knowing she had to break the tempting contact. For too many days, they hadn't touched.

She was convinced now that Brendan had Diego in some kind of hold. He was too strong, too self-confident, to let anyone command him; therefore, the hold had to be…personal.

"Why do you have to go out? Brendan will be with his wife."

"Leave it alone, Magnolia."

She crossed her arms. "Well, that's progress. You didn't tell me not to worry my pretty little head about it."

"If I'd thought I would live to tell about it, I would have."

She smiled reluctantly. She wanted the awkwardness between them to end. She wanted the ease they'd found with each other during the first two weeks of their marriage, before they'd lost their heads and made love. Before everything had changed.

She leaned closer to whisper dramatically. "Are you a leather-and-chains man, honey?"

He gave her a lopsided grin. "I can't say that I am."

"You can't say, or you're not?"

"I'm not."

"Good. I didn't think so, but then, who would have thought Judge Shaunnessey…"

"I think that is a matter of who, not what."

"As it should be. Listen, since tomorrow's Saturday and I don't have school, you can sleep in. Just leave the car keys on the table for me so I can go shopping in the morning."

"Hey, Maggie." Ruthie, her fellow waitress stuck her head

around the corner and whispered loudly, "I'm taking half of your tips."

"Be right there." She sent one last serious look Diego's way. "Just be careful."

"I always am, *novia.*"

Maggie couldn't find his car keys anywhere, so they had to be in his bedroom. She glanced at the mantel clock. Nine a.m. She knew he hadn't come home until almost three. She didn't want to wake him, but she wanted to get her grocery shopping done so she could spend the afternoon with Jasmine and the baby.

Lord, she was tired. She eyed Diego's closed bedroom door. She wouldn't mind crawling under the blankets with him and sleeping a while.

She shook her head. She really needed to spend some time away from the apartment by herself. For that she needed car keys.

She opened the door to his room as quietly as she could and peeked in. When the lump under the quilt didn't move, she tiptoed in, searching the room with her eyes. Not seeing the keys, she headed to the chair where he'd draped his jeans. She lifted the pants, slid her fingers into the right hand pocket—

"You'd make a lousy spy," came the sleep-roughened voice before he rolled over and looked at her. "Did you know you sigh very loudly when you're irritated?"

She dropped the pants. Her face heated. "Then I must spend a lot of time sighing these days."

He grinned. Slowly, it faded to a frown. He sat up. "Come here."

"No."

"I won't bite."

"Don't order me."

"Come here, please, Magnolia." He patted the bed beside him.

Maggie sat, tucking a leg under her. He cupped her chin and stared into her eyes.

"Are you ill?"

"No, why?"

"You don't look yourself."

She tugged out of his grasp. "I'm tired, that's all."

He placed his palm on her forehead. "You're warm."

"I'm fine. I need your car keys so that I can go to the store. I told you last night."

"I'll drive you."

Maggie shot off the bed. "I want to go alone." She enunciated each word distinctly. "I'm tired of you dogging my steps, Diego. I need some time by myself. Besides, when you're along, we spend twice as much money as we should. You're an impulse buyer."

"It's the first time I've enjoyed shopping," he said mildly, watching her too closely for her comfort. "I've learned a lot about what to look for when selecting produce and meat. You would deny me another lesson?"

"Oh, right. You couldn't care less about going to the grocery store. What's the real reason?"

"I like shopping with you. That's the real reason, Magnolia."

The sincerity on his face irritated her as much as it flattered her. She threw up her hands. "All right. I give up. Get your butt—" she paused to flash him a sultry smile, the memory of him vivid in her mind "—your very nice butt, by the way, in the shower. I'm not sitting around all morning waiting for you."

"You are ill," J.D. announced when they got back from the store. He set down the bags of groceries he carried, set hers aside, as well, then touched her forehead, knowing already that she was feverish. Her eyes were glazed, her face flushed. "*Dios,* Magnolia. You're burning up."

"I don't feel so good," she said in a tiny voice, reaching

for the counter for support. "Must be that flu that's been going around school."

He lifted her into his arms and she collapsed against him. The heat from her penetrated his clothes and warmed his own skin.

Standing her beside her bed, he pulled back the covers and fluffed two pillows. When he turned back to her, he saw she was trying to toe off her shoes.

"Sit," he said.

"Don't order me." She sat, anyway.

"I should have had 'obey' put into the marriage vows," he muttered as he crouched before her and slipped her shoes off.

"Wouldn't have mattered. You promised to love and you don't. I could have promised to obey and had it mean as little."

He held the socks he'd just removed as he looked at her. She was sitting up but her eyes were closed and she swayed a little. Guilt. Just what he needed on top of everything else he was dealing with.

"Sorry," she whispered. "I didn't mean that."

But she had. He knew she had.

"What do you want to wear?" he asked, ignoring everything else.

"Could I wear a T-shirt of yours?"

He pulled a T-shirt from a drawer and helped her undress, sliding the shirt over her head before removing her bra. His hands brushed her body, felt the warmth. She kept her eyes closed the whole time.

"Do you have a thermometer?" he asked.

"Mmm-hmm." She fell against the pillows and sighed. "Cool."

He pushed most of the bedding to the foot of the bed, leaving just the sheet over her. From the bathroom he got the thermometer and stuck it in her mouth, holding it there as she seemed to drift to sleep. He pulled it out and angled it until he could see what it registered—100.6. Not as bad as he'd feared, but bad enough. He brushed her hair from her face, watched her snuggle deeper into the pillows.

After a few minutes, he left her to call his doctor's office and get instructions on how to care for her. He filled a pitcher with water and set it beside her bed, woke her up to drink some and take some aspirin. Then he called a substitute waitress and tried to get out of work himself. The manager of the club told him he could let him leave at ten o'clock, no earlier.

He'd never taken care of anyone before. He sat beside her watching her sleep, wondering at the feelings of tenderness and worry. Of course she'd gotten under his skin. He'd known she would. But he'd thought it would be just a physical irritation, not one that would tug at something deeper inside him.

It won't work, he reminded himself. She's a homebody; you can't be. The Grand Canyon divided them with their differences.

After a while, he noted a light sheen of perspiration coating her face, then she shivered. He tugged the quilt up, holding it under her chin until she stopped shaking. He dialed Jasmine, not intending to ask her to come stay with her sister while he worked, but perhaps Raine would come. He got the answering machine.

Who else could he call?

She stirred and opened her eyes, then shut them again. "My eyes hurt," she said.

"One of the possible symptoms, according to the doctor. Here, drink some water."

She sipped and fell back against the pillows. "Actually, I feel a little better. I could eat something. Maybe it was just exhaustion."

"Exhaustion doesn't spike a fever, *novia*. Have we got soup?"

We. The word shouted joyously in Maggie's head. It was the first time he'd said it other than in regards to where they were going or what they were doing. Yes, *we* have soup in *our* cupboard in *our* kitchen, she wanted to sing.

"Chicken noodle. In the cupboard by the refrigerator," she said.

"I'll be right back. Drink some more water, if you can."

She slept some more, argued with him that she didn't need anyone staying with her, convinced him to bring the television into her bedroom so she could listen to it at least, then ordered him to go to work.

"I will be home by ten-fifteen," he said, the worry coming through in his voice.

"Okay. Thank you for everything."

"Sleep, Magnolia. It's the best thing for you."

"I will." She opened her eyes long enough to see the expression of concern on his face. "You can call, honey. I won't accuse you of checkin' up on me."

"Good. All right. Good." His relief was palpable. "Sleep well."

Maggie drifted in and out of sleep all evening, waking when Diego called, drinking water, watching television through slitted eyes until they grew heavy and she slept again. Close to ten o'clock she woke up more fully, the old black-and-white movie catching her interest. When he got home, she ran her fingers through her hair to comb it and struggled to pull herself up.

He came through her doorway. She shut her eyes after the effort of sitting.

"Just when had you planned on telling me about your secret life, Diego?"

Twelve

J.D. halted, then moved forward hesitantly. What the hell had happened while he was gone?

"I always suspected you had a dual identity," she added, glancing at him briefly. "I'm really hurt that you made me find out on my own, instead of your telling me. Hmmpf. Mild-mannered maître d' by day and mystery man by night. I should have guessed."

"Should you have?"

"I feel like an idiot for not having known."

He sat beside her and touched her forehead. Warm, but enough to be delirious? He didn't know. "Would you explain what you're talking about, Magnolia?"

"Zorro."

"*What?*"

She opened one eye and pointed to the television. "Do you know Zorro's real name?"

"Ah, no. I don't think I've ever—"

"Diego. 'Course, you're much better looking than he is."

J.D. spun around to stare at the television.

"We will return to *The Mark of Zorro* starring Tyrone Power and Linda Darnell after these messages," the disembodied announcer said.

He rubbed his forehead, relaxing. She didn't know, after all. Zorro. *Dios.*

"How do you feel?" he asked.

"Like a cornflake."

"Can I get you anything?" He fluffed pillows around her. "Milk? A bowl?"

She smiled. "A cold, wet washcloth would be nice."

He made her take more aspirin and drink a full glass of water, then he gathered a bowl of water and two washcloths. He turned off the television and the bedroom lamp, leaving only the bathroom light to illuminate the room, enough to see her, but not enough to bother her eyes. He sat beside her on the bed, wrung out a washcloth and folded it twice.

"Tell me a story," she said.

"What kind of a story?"

"A fairy tale." She sighed as he laid the cloth on her forehead. "About a princess and a frog."

He smiled at the way she wriggled into her pillows, awaiting a bedtime story. After a minute, he turned over the washcloth, giving her a cool side, noting how quickly the water had evaporated. She sighed again.

"Once upon a time," she prompted.

He hoped she wouldn't remember any of this in the morning. "Once upon a time," he began, "there was a beautiful princess—"

"But lonely."

"What?"

"The princess is always beautiful, but lonely."

"Oh. Okay." He replaced the washcloth with a fresh one. "Once upon a time, there was a beautiful but lonely princess."

"*Young* princess."

He made an impatient sound. "A beautiful but lonely princess who should have been married years ago but who interrupted her suitors so much, they were never actually able to propose.''

Maggie grinned.

"This princess believed that the man she married would be perfect in every way. The problem was, no man could live up to her expectations.''

"Why? What did she want that was so outrageous?''

"Oh, she had a list. Tall, dark and handsome. Good sense of humor. A snazzy dresser. Rich enough not to need her dowry.''

"Doesn't seem like too much to me,'' she said, then softened it with a smile. "Go on, please.''

"The princess found herself alone more and more as the eligible men in her kingdom and the neighboring kingdoms married women who loved them, flaws and all. Then on her thirtieth birthday, she decided to visit her grandmother, who lived a full day's ride from the castle.'' He flipped the washcloth again, alarmed by how warm it had gotten in such a brief amount of time. "Along the way to Grandma's house, the princess and her servants stopped to have a picnic lunch beside a pond. Of course, because she was the princess, she ate alone while the servants ate together a distance away. She envied the way they laughed and talked together, and wished someone would come along who she could talk to. Suddenly, a frog landed smack in the middle of her potato salad.''

"Yuk.''

"He was quite clean, you know. Spent all of his days in water.''

"Covered with pond scum.''

J.D. switched washcloths again as her face flushed even more. He skimmed his fingers down her arm as it rested on top of the sheet. She radiated fire. "Who's telling this story?''

"I'll be quiet.''

"The frog croaked at her, which was more conversation than she'd had all morning. She was so grateful to the little green guy that she leaned over and kissed him.''

"And he turned into a handsome prince.''

"Not quite."

Maggie opened her eyes to a squint.

"Your version's been done to death," he said. "In my story, the princess turns into a frog."

She laughed. "Why am I not surprised? The machismo version. I don't think that was what the princess had in mind, but go on."

"You promised to be quiet."

"I'll try harder."

"Thank you. Needless to say, the princess was so shocked to find herself perched upon a mound of potato salad alongside this good-looking frog, her crown slipped down over one eye. The gallant frog used his talented tongue to set the crown aright and the princess croaked her thanks. 'How 'bout a swim in my pond, Princess?' the frog asked. 'I never learned how,' she demurred. 'Princesses never have any fun. It's a royal rule.' The frog assured her he would teach her, and off they went, leaping one over the other, until they reached the water's edge."

He wiped Maggie's arms gently with a wet washcloth, then dipped it in water again and pressed it to her throat. She sucked in a breath but said nothing. "Now, the princess liked adventure as much as the next person, and for a while everything was wonderful. After all, in the frog world, he was considered tall, dark and handsome, so the princess had no complaints there."

"Lucky princess."

"She thought so, too. The frog protected her from the dangers of the pond. They shared a lily pad in perfect harmony. As the sun beat upon them, the water soothed their skin. All day they swam and floated. A breeze blew. The trees shaded them from the sun."

"That feels heavenly," she whispered as he changed cloths.

He could feel her body cooling. "Life was good for the princess and the frog. They seemed compatible enough. Then the frog, being gallant, caught a fly for her dinner."

"Oh, double yuk."

"But try as he would, he couldn't convince the poor princess to swallow it. He tried again and again. He knew her survival hinged on her living *his* life, the life of a frog. She had to learn to eat flies. She just had to. Here, drink some water," he said to Maggie, helping her sit up and holding the glass to her lips. When she leaned back, exhausted, he applied more cool cloths and continued his story. "The frog was a realist, however, and he soon saw she wouldn't survive life in the pond. He had to do something, fast."

"Did they love each other?"

Quiet settled in the room as he considered her question. "They came from different worlds, and their relationship wasn't destined to be. So the frog found the courage to kiss the princess and, poof, she was human again. She sat in the pond, a lily pad snagged on her crown, and she was—"

"Crying," Maggie said, turning onto her side so he couldn't see her expression. "This is too sad of a story, Diego. Fairy tales are supposed to end happily."

"It does. She was glad for the experience because the frog had taught her something important."

"What? That eating flies is a matter of life or death?"

"That what seems right at the time, isn't necessarily right forever." He stroked her arm with the cloth. "The princess climbed into her carriage a sadder but wiser woman. Then at the crossroad to Grandma's house, a carriage wheel broke, halting their progress. And who should come along but a chivalrous stranger who helped them fix the wheel, not worrying a bit about dirtying his garments, then accompanying them to Grandma's. She watched him astride his horse as he rode beside the carriage. He wasn't tall, dark and handsome, but he was kind and his eyes twinkled when he smiled. And he told her he loved children, wanted a bunch of them himself. She thought him Prince Charming. So they married and lived happily ever after."

"But what about the frog?"

"The frog never forgot the princess, even when he settled

down with a lady frog who didn't mind moving lily pad to lily pad.''

"He never forgot the princess?''

"Never.''

J.D. watched her tuck her hands under her cheek. She was quiet for a long time. Then finally she spoke, her voice slurred with impending sleep.

"Did they ever make love?''

He swallowed. "Once. Just once.''

"I'll bet she thought it was the most beautiful experience of her life.''

He waited until he thought she was asleep, then he pressed his lips to her temple. Her temperature had dropped some.

"I would've learned to like flies,'' she murmured.

"I can't believe you went running this morning,'' Maggie said. They'd just gotten home after Diego had picked her up from school, still dressed in his running clothes.

"I am not sick,'' he mumbled.

"Is that so?''

"I do not get sick.''

She pulled out the thermometer from his mouth and read it. "This doesn't lie, Zorro—101.2.''

"Do not call me Zorro. It is worse than 'honey.' And I have never been sick.''

"Everyone catches the occasional cold or flu.''

"I do not.''

She laid the thermometer on the nightstand beside his bed. He was stretched out on top of the quilt, his face flushed, his eyes as glazed as hers must have been a few days ago, except that his symptoms were undoubtedly intensified by irritation.

"What's the matter? Afraid you can't prowl the streets for a few nights?'' She slashed a Z in the air with an imaginary sword. "They'll just have to do without you for a little while.''

She felt so close to him, so needed, finally. He could talk about how their marriage wasn't real until he was hoarse; she saw it differently. He may have tried to tell her again in the fairy tale he'd created when she was sick, but she wasn't buying it. The princess not being able to survive life in the pond seemed a flimsy excuse.

"I'm going to get you some aspirin and water, then I'll arrange substitutes for both of us at work tonight."

"I am going to work." He swung his legs over the edge of the bed and stood up. *"Dios."* He dropped back down.

"Dizzy?" she asked sweetly.

His eyes closed; he nodded reluctantly.

She knelt to take off his shoes. "Do you need help undressing?"

He shook his head.

"I'll be back in a few minutes."

J.D. listened to the sound of the door shutting. He tugged at his clothes until they lay in a heap next to his feet, then he slid under the blankets and gratefully relaxed. In truth, he was glad she'd taken over. He couldn't remember feeling so bad. Worse, he liked her fussing over him, liked it far too much.

He needed to call Callahan and let him know what was going on. The discovery that Hastings was afraid of his wife had led to some surprising revelations, the most important being that Hastings wasn't the head man in the operation, as they'd believed. The knowledge gave them an advantage they'd never had before, even as it presented a new problem—how to get to the man in charge.

J.D. punched in Callahan's number and waited, the receiver cushioned by his pillow so that he didn't have to hold it.

"I've got the flu," he said without preface.

"Bad?"

"If it's like Magnolia's, I'll be down a couple of days."

"Did you have a meeting scheduled tonight?"

"Tentatively. Let's just play this by ear. It's not a good idea to show any weakness."

"All right. Stay in touch."

He used the remainder of his energy to cradle the receiver as Maggie returned.

"We're all set for tonight," she said, handing him the pills and pouring a glass of water. "Who was that on the phone?"

"My father."

"Ah. The Zorro of the senior set. Do you come from a long line of mystery men?"

He took the medicine, then lay back, ignoring her as he pulled the quilt over his shoulders. She dragged it higher. "Would you like some cool washcloths?"

"I just need to sleep."

"Dismissed, am I?" she asked cheerfully.

He opened an eye. "Thank you, Magnolia. You've been very helpful."

"You know, Diego, you could accept my help with a little more grace. I let you take care of me."

"I'm not as sick as you."

"Uh-huh. Okay, I'll let you sleep. But just let me know if you need anything."

"I will."

She wished she knew Spanish. She might have learned a lot about her husband as he spoke in his sleep, the fever freeing his words. His voice held her mesmerized—commanding, cynical and questioning, a how-dare-you-speak-to-me-like-that tone. What could he be saying?

Her curiosity getting the best of her, she found her tape recorder and taped his one-sided conversation until his eyes flew open and he grabbed her by the shirt, pulling her close to his face.

"No le tengas confianza."

"Shh, Diego. It's all right."

"¿Sabes lo que él hubiera hecho contigo?"

He rambled some more, his expression fierce, his tone arrogant. This was a man she didn't know at all.

She needed to stop his words, the words of a stranger. "Here, drink."

He pushed her hand away, spilling water in an arc from the bed to the nightstand, then he grabbed her shirt again. He seemed to stare right at her. *"Haces de mi trabajo mucho más difícil. No debería hacer sido de esta manera, Magnolia. Dios, quisiera nuna haberte conocido."*

He fell against the pillows, his mouth twisted in anguish. Maggie wrung out a facecloth and laid it on his forehead. With another one, she cooled his chest and arms.

"Magnolia."

She looked at his face and saw signs of awareness. She refilled his water glass and passed it to him, hiding the tape recorder at the same time. As he drank, he examined her face, then her shirt, where his hands had twisted the fabric. He set the glass aside.

"Did I hurt you?" he asked quietly.

"Of course not." She fussed with the quilt. As sick as he was, she couldn't keep her eyes off his chest. She couldn't keep her memory off the brief, beautiful moment they'd shared just a few days ago. Suddenly, it seemed like a lifetime ago. Another person ago.

He laid his hand, warm and dry, on hers. "Did I say something to offend you?"

She pushed herself off the bed and picked up the pitcher, intending to refill it. "I have no idea what you said. You spoke in Spanish."

By the time she returned he was asleep again, resting calmly this time, his breathing slow and even. She put a hand on his forehead. The fever had broken.

Glancing at the floor beside the nightstand, she contemplated the tape recorder tucked away there. She let the inevitable guilt drift over her, then waited until it passed. If she had to find out about him by trickery, so be it. At least now she would know what she was fighting.

Maggie refused to believe that Diego was involved. She looked at everything and nothing as she made her way blindly from the student union to the parking lot where he always picked her up. A friend had just translated the tape for her. From it, she'd learned that Diego was working for Brendan

Hastings, and that huge sums of money were involved. Mind-boggling sums. Millions.

Her stomach churned, just thinking about it. She couldn't be that wrong about him. She couldn't. Brendan had to be forcing him in some way.

"I wish I'd never met you."

His final words in his delirium twisted the knot inside her tighter. There was no doubt he'd meant her. *He wished he'd never met her.* How was she supposed to live with that knowledge? She'd have to let him go. For his sake. For his happiness. She'd thought she was prepared to do anything for him. But…give him up? She didn't know if she was strong enough.

"Magnolia?"

He was there, standing before her, looking curious, and concerned, and…tender. She dropped her book bag to the ground and hugged him.

His arms came around her, a sanctuary of warmth and strength and safekeeping.

"What's wrong?" he asked close to her ear, his hand stroking her hair.

I love you. Why couldn't she tell him that? Because when he'd grabbed her shirt and spoken to her in his delirium, one of the things he'd said was that she made his job much more difficult. She'd made a mess of his life. Or—he'd made a mess of his life, and she'd made it worse.

She bit back a sob. She couldn't give him up. She couldn't.

"I'm not wrong about you," she whispered.

"About what?"

She squeezed him tighter. "Let's run away. Let's go someplace else and start a whole new life."

"What?" J.D. leaned back to look at her. He'd known she was upset about something just by the way she'd walked toward the parking lot, veering away from where he waited. She hadn't even seen him get out of the car and hurry to divert her.

She curved her fingers into his forearms. "We can find a

little town somewhere. Doesn't that sound great? Just you and me?''

He put his palm on her forehead, fearing she'd had a relapse.

''I'm not sick. We need to talk. And this time you're not going to ignore my questions. This time I need the truth. No matter how much it hurts.''

''All right,'' he said slowly. ''Let's go home.''

He closed the car door after she climbed in, then walked around to the driver's side. He slid the key into the ignition.

The back doors opened and two men swung in, one from each side. The steel barrel of a revolver pressed icily against his neck. He noted the frozen fear in Magnolia's eyes before he looked in the rearview mirror at the man behind him.

''Drive,'' came the order from the back seat.

''Where?''

''Just get us out of the parking lot. I'll tell you where as we go.''

J.D. followed the same path he'd driven for almost two weeks as they left the campus and turned right. He glanced at Magnolia and noted the way her fingers dug into the upholstery and her wide eyes focused on him. He stared at her intently, taking her measure. Why wasn't she asking questions? Why was she accepting—perhaps even expecting—what was happening?

He gave her a small, encouraging smile.

She offered a hesitant one in return.

He nodded, satisfied. She wouldn't panic.

Thirteen

Wherever they'd been brought, it was cold. Bone-chilling cold. Or maybe it was fear that caused Maggie's teeth to chatter and her limbs to shake. At some point, she and Diego had been blindfolded, gagged and made to lie down in the back seat of the car, their hands tied behind them, before continuing on a drive that lasted another twenty minutes or so. They'd been hauled from the car and shoved up some creaky stairs into a building.

"Take off their restraints."

Maggie turned toward the voice. Brendan Hastings? But...if Diego worked for Brendan, why would he kidnap them? It didn't make sense. Nothing made sense. When the men had climbed into the car, she'd assumed they were Brendan's enemies and that Diego was the target. But now—

She jumped as icy fingers fumbled with the rope around her hands. She shoved off the blindfold and sought Diego. Relieved that he was only a few feet away, she peeled the duct tape slowly from across her mouth and watched him do the same, his eyes cautioning her to silence.

"Ah, I do love the telepathic communication between husband and wife," Brendan said, an expansive smile on his face. "Fascinating, isn't it?"

Maggie glanced around quickly, seeing a boarded-up, dilapidated room with rotting floorboards and a layer of dirt coating everything. She flinched as something slightly smaller than a cat scurried along the wall. She stepped closer to her husband, away from Tweedledee, who, along with Tweedledum, must have been waiting with Brendan.

"Go ahead, my dear. You may stand near your husband."

She refused to give Brendan the pleasure of showing any weakness, so she didn't cling to Diego, although she did move next to him. She straightened her spine, tossed back her hair and waited.

"What's going on, Mr. Hastings?" Diego asked, resting his hand on her lower back.

The gesture was almost her undoing. It conveyed his concern, his attempt to protect her and his need to be in charge, all at once. She drew a breath and settled herself.

"I have a bit of a problem, Duran." He flicked his fingers down his jacket sleeve, brushing at something only he could see. "Our last transaction wasn't deposited."

"That's impossible," Diego said.

"I assure you, it didn't happen."

A door opened and the two men who'd snatched Diego and Maggie came in. One handed Maggie's book bag to Brendan; the other plopped a paper sack on the floor. It tipped over, spilling an assortment of items into the dust. Brendan moved things with the toe of his shoe.

"That's everything, boss."

"Good. Dump the car, then get back here. I'll need you to watch over Mrs. Duran while Mr. Duran and I take a little drive."

J.D. slid his hand to her waist and squeezed as he felt her react to Hastings's words. *Dios*, he was proud of her. Amaz-

ingly, she hadn't said a word. He would have expected her to
challenge Hastings about why they were there, at the least.
"Where are we going?" he asked.

"We're going to find out where my money went."

"Do you think if I'd cheated on you, I'd still be in town?"

"Your pretty little wife doesn't seem to be surprised at our
conversation. So she does know what you do for a living, after
all, Duran?"

"I know," she said, startling J.D.

"And approve?"

"A man's gotta make a living."

Brendan chuckled. "You sound like a gangster's moll from
a forties' movie, my dear. Stand by your man—wouldn't that
be a little more appropriate for the nineties?"

Maggie pursed her lips. In truth, her only knowledge of
criminals came from the movies she watched, but she'd be
damned if she'd give up without a fight. With all her heart,
she knew Diego wasn't like Brendan.

"I'm to be insurance, I suppose," Maggie said. Diego's
fingers dug into her. "My husband's word is his bond, Mr.
Hastings."

"Such a devoted little wife you have, Duran."

"I'm a lucky man."

"Indeed you are." Brendan plucked Diego's pager from the
pile on the floor. It had been taken from him, along with his
gun, when they'd been forced into the back seat of the car.
Brendan fidgeted with the casing until he tripped a panel, revealing a tiny audiocassette. He dumped it into his palm.
"What have we here? Blackmail? What do you think now,
my dear? Do you still believe he's an honest man?"

"And a cautious one," she said.

He grinned at her, then at Diego. "Brains and beauty. I envy
you." He tucked the cassette and pager into a pocket, then
opened Maggie's book bag. He withdrew her own pager and
toyed with it. Apparently satisfied that it contained nothing
unusual, he turned it off and set it aside.

He dug deeper into the bag and came up with her cassette player.

"I just use it to take notes in class," Maggie said, panic striking her. "Spanish class."

Brendan contemplated her a few seconds, then cocked his head. "What's got your wife in a dither, Duran?"

"Probably the fact she's being held against her will."

"Hmm. I wonder." He examined the recorder. "Let's just see what's on here, why don't we?"

Maggie thought she was going to be sick. Diego's voice came across the tiny speaker clearly. She felt him tense behind her. His hand loosened, then fell away as he heard himself reveal too much information about his business with Brendan. They listened to the end. Maggie could translate the words in her head now that she knew them.

She wanted to die.

"Don't trust him," Diego had ordered her in Spanish after grabbing her shirt and pulling her to him.

"Shh, Diego. It's all right."

"Do you know what he would have done with you?"

Maggie got lost in the next part, where he talked of huge sums of money and dirty bankers and Swiss accounts.

"Here, drink."

"You make my job so much more difficult. It wasn't supposed to be like this, Magnolia. God, I wish I'd never met you." The anguish in his voice pierced her once again.

The tape stopped.

"So, all is not what it appears in the Duran household," Brendan said in delight, obviously having no trouble translating the words. "I'm a little confused, however. Were you talking in your sleep?"

Maggie glanced at Diego. He wouldn't even look at her. He'd retreated from her as effectively as if he'd left the room.

Brendan dumped the recorder into her book bag and tossed it to Dum. "Put that and the rest of Duran's things in the car." He faced Diego, looking smug. "I imagine you have some final words for your wife. The Bard says it best, doesn't he? 'Parting is such sweet sorrow.'"

When the door closed, Diego grabbed her by the arms and held her in front of him.

"I'm sor—"

"Be quiet and listen to me," he whispered harshly. "I am a special agent for the FBI."

Maggie went rigid. *"What?"*

He stepped away from her to tug at a floorboard. "My cover has been blown. The deposit Hastings refers to was made. He's just saying that as an excuse to get rid of me. Who knows what he plans for you."

Shock held her speechless as he worked the board back and forth.

"There was a directional beeper in my car and in your pager. Now the car is gone and the pager is turned off. A man named Novacek will have seen us taken from campus. With any luck the satellite signals were transmitted and received before they were lost." The wood splintered, sounding like cannon fire. "Our last hope is your necklace."

She clutched her pendant, bewildered.

He gripped another board. "The device that's in your pendant is recharged by body heat, but it's also experimental. I checked it a few days ago and it was working, so that's a good sign. However, the signal is not nearly as powerful as the other devices." When the board wouldn't budge, he tried another. "I've done everything I could to keep you safe and help you be rescued. Have faith that you'll be found."

Maggie swallowed. "What about you?"

"I always knew the risks."

"But—"

Giving up freeing a second floorboard, he passed her the first one. "You have to take Hastings out with one swing. You won't get a second chance. Straight into the face, all right? Straight in."

"I don't—"

He dragged her to the front door. "I'll take the others."

Terrified, she gripped the board like a baseball bat. Wildly, she sought his eyes at the sound of someone stepping onto the creaking wood outside.

"You can do this, Magnolia."

She shifted foot to foot, finding a stronghold, then went still. She gritted her teeth. She raised the board high. She pulled in a deep breath.

The door opened.

The sickening thud of wood connecting with Brendan's face sent her stomach somersaulting. She stared in shock as the man crumpled. Blood spilled onto the floor beneath his face. Choking back her nausea, she lifted her head and saw Diego grappling with Dum.

She screamed his name as Dee pulled a gun from inside his jacket.

"Nooooo." She swung the board, connecting, sending the gun sailing. Diego slammed Dum against the wall. He sank like a rag doll to the floor.

Dee charged him. Diego jumped aside. Dee fell face-first, rolled once and came up aiming another gun.

"Get behind me," Diego ordered Maggie as she screeched.

She heaved the board against the opposite wall. Dee turned at the clatter. Diego lunged. They fell to the floor, Diego sprawled on top of the huge man, his fingers a vise on Dee's wrist. Their hands shook; the gun vibrated. The room echoed with primal male sounds.

With a grunt, Maggie stomped on Dee's hand and the weapon dropped out of suddenly limp fingers. She kicked it out of reach, ran to grab it, then pointed it at Dee as Diego rolled away and stood.

"A gun in an amateur's hand is nothing to challenge," Diego cautioned, breathing hard, as Dee dragged himself to his knees.

Maggie passed the shaking weapon to Diego. Behind them the door burst open and a group of men wearing blue windbreakers stormed the room.

"Timing could have been a little better, Cal," Diego said, the lightness in his voice making Maggie gape at him.

"Every time we locked on a signal, it died. The necklace worked, J.D. It worked."

Maggie stared at the scene. The men in matching jackets were dragging a bloody-faced Brendan and his cohorts to their feet.

Her gaze drifted to Diego. She saw his mouth move. He was talking but she couldn't hear his words. Wind rushed through her head, loud, unrelenting, cold. Achingly cold.

Numb, she watched him finally look her way. She thought she read her name on his lips.

He hurried toward her as she reached an unsteady hand to him.

"We're safe?" she asked. It took him forever to get to her.

"We're safe," he mouthed.

"Madre de Dios," she said. Then she fainted.

Maggie paced. Back and forth, back and forth she moved across the small interrogation room, as she had done for much of the four hours she'd been waiting. Diego had offered to have her driven home, but she was afraid if she accepted, he wouldn't come see her. At least this way, he had to face her.

The food someone had brought her went untouched. She sipped occasionally at a glass of ice water that had long since warmed to room temperature. She was tired and scared and suddenly very lonely. She stopped pacing and dropped into a chair, shoving her hair from her face, then letting it fall forward again as she rested her elbows on the table.

The door opened. She lifted her head and watched Diego come quietly into the room and shut the door. He pulled out a chair on the opposite side of the table.

"How are your hands?"

She stared at the bandages covering deep wounds where wood splinters had gouged her. "They're okay."

His cool professionalism cut into her. When she'd come out of the first faint of her life, he'd been holding her, but there was a distance between them that seemed insurmountable. She'd tape-recorded him—that had hurt him. He hadn't trusted her—that had hurt her.

"Is Brendan done spilling his guts?" she asked, trying to stay as cool as he.

"He's still cooperating. He's much more afraid of what his father-in-law could do to him than what we could. He's full of information."

"I take it he was afraid of his wife because he was afraid of her father, who must run things?"

"Yes. The father has already been picked up. More arrests are expected. People's silence is often bought with threats. Many will talk to us willingly, in exchange for deals and protection. What we've uncovered is a nationwide network beyond the small area over which Hastings reigned. Most involve drugs, therefore, a variety of offenses. And the IRS will take part, as well."

"So this was a big case?"

"It didn't start that way. It began when a young seamstress of Misty's disappeared." He tipped his chair back on two legs. "There was no trail to follow. She was without family and new to San Francisco. Months later she called Misty, hysterical. She'd gotten away, but she was in Miami and without a cent."

Maggie leaned forward, caught up in the story. "Why didn't she go to the police?"

"She was afraid to. She had heard that some of them were involved in the prostitution ring. She didn't know who she could trust. So, Misty flew to Miami and brought her home."

"Misty called the FBI?"

"No. She contacted the only person she trusted implicitly."

"Judge Shaunnessey."

"Yes."

"How did she know him?"

"They met a long, long time ago, when he was a public defender. The facts are for Misty to tell, not me. Anyway, he called us. The girl didn't know who had taken her. The only potential suspect was Hastings. They'd met in a bar one night. He had taken her to his penthouse. A week later, she was abducted. She kept her wits about her, did what she was told, and therefore avoided the drugs that are given to those who won't cooperate. She heard whispers from others that two women had been killed when they'd fought back. She just bided her time."

"Is she all right now?"

"She's anxious to testify."

Maggie's gaze drifted over him. She wished she could soothe the weariness from his face. She wished he would hold her and tell her everything was going to be all right.

"How were you involved?" she asked him instead.

"San Francisco was a new market for him. He got careless, thinking himself to be unknown here, so he met openly with people known to facilitate money laundering. Some of them are members at the Carola."

"*What?*"

"In exchange for reduced charges, we convinced one of his contacts to recommend me as a facilitator. The details are not important. It took patience to wait him out. He made his first contact with me when he showed up at the Carola as a new member, but he continued to put me off. Unfortunately, you caught his eye."

"Would he have used me for...for—"

"He would have attempted to make you his mistress certainly. He admired you greatly."

"Gosh, I'm so flattered."

A fleeting smile crossed his lips.

"What about when he got tired of me?"

"I don't know. You're older than they like."

"Oh, stop, Diego. I can't take all this flattery at once."

"You're bright," he continued. "He may have let you return to your own life—if you didn't know too much. He may also have found a place for you in his business. Like the others, he would have kept you in line with drugs, or threats to your family. Or he might have killed you if you'd resisted too strongly.''

Maggie folded her hands on the table to steady them. ''Don't hold back, now. You can give it to me straight.''

''It doesn't serve either of us to pretend any longer, does it?'' He let his chair drop onto all four legs.

''How long have you been an FBI agent?''

''Three years. I got a bachelor's degree in criminology from Berkeley, then I worked in a crime lab analyzing data. I was accepted to the academy the first time I applied.''

''Why didn't you tell me you were an agent?''

''I was undercover.''

''Surely other agents are married and go undercover. Their wives must know.''

''I believed that the less you knew, the safer you were.''

She shook her head. ''You didn't trust me.''

''I could not share with you. It could have jeopardized the entire operation. I knew it was winding down. I did not think I would have to keep the secret for long.''

''But I'm your wife.''

J.D. hesitated. He leaned back and crossed his arms. ''No.'' He watched her face pale. ''I'm not your wife?''

''The marriage license was as phony as the rest of my ID. Duran isn't my name.''

''Duran isn't… I'm not…'' She flattened her hands on the table. ''What *is* your name?''

''Shaunnessey.''

''Shaunnessey,'' she repeated dully. ''The judge—''

''Is my father.''

Her expressive face revealed everything—shock, hurt, growing anger. Similar to how he felt when he'd realized she'd tape-recorded him without his knowledge.

''Well, that simplifies things, doesn't it? No divorce, no annulment, no legal mess whatsoever,'' she said, shoving away from the table and standing. She picked up her glass of water and turned her back on him, but not before he saw the glass almost shake loose from her hand.

"I did stop Hastings from having you."

"Thank you."

Her blatantly sarcastic tone attempted to put him in his place. He wouldn't let it.

"I was protecting you, Magnolia. If nothing else, give me credit for that."

Maggie slammed the glass on the table. "You don't think I could have gotten myself out of that situation if I'd had knowledge beyond the little you shared? You think I married you because I thought I needed to be protected?"

"Didn't you?"

"Silly me, I thought I married you to give us a chance to know each other. If you were honest with yourself, you'd admit that you offered marriage not because I needed help but because you wanted to be with me, too."

"I was keeping you out of Hastings's reach."

She lifted her chin. "I don't believe you would have offered marriage as a solution to another woman. I believe you offered it to me because you wanted me. There has always been something strong between us. This was a way to indulge your fantasy."

He scowled. "I was protecting you. And look how you paid me back. By secretly recording me like some criminal."

She had no answer to that. "I need to go home," she said, picking up her book bag and starting out of the room. He blocked her path.

"We have an issue remaining, Magnolia."

"Drop me a note."

"We made love."

"We had sex." She let her words hang in the air, cold, hard, accusing. "I absolve you, Diego."

"We did not use birth control."

"Well, don't sweat it, honey. Jazz won't come after you with a shotgun."

"If you are pregnant, I deserve to know." His hands fisted. "A child deserves a father. I did not grow up with mine. I know what that is like."

Maggie closed her eyes. She wanted her love for him to die a sudden death. Instead, it was being kept alive by life support, waiting for her to give him the words that would decide their fate.

"I'll be in touch with you in three weeks," he said into her silence. "You should know by then, right?"

I know now. The words hid behind her own cowardice. He was crowding her, standing so close she could hear him breathe. So close she couldn't take a deep breath herself. She couldn't show any weakness, especially now.

He curved a hand around her arm. "Will you tell me the truth?"

Maggie swallowed hard. Was this the last time she would feel his touch? Oh, God, how could she survive the rest of her life without it? She wanted to hate him for his secrets, for his willpower to keep them. She didn't hate him—couldn't hate him.

So this is what dying feels like. There wasn't a light waiting, drawing her in. There was just darkness and cold and loneliness.

"I'll tell you the truth," she said, lifting her chin.

He let go of her with his hand but not his gaze. "I'll drive you home," he said after a minute.

"I'll see myself home, thank you."

"I'll drive you."

She shrugged. "Suit yourself."

The ride was short and silent. He pulled up in front of her apartment.

"You can pick up your things anytime," she said in a monotone. "Just come when you know I'm not here. Give Jazz the key when you're done."

"Magnolia—"

She cut him off with a gesture. "Don't use that soothing tone with me. This is the most painful thing I've ever, *ever* done. I'm sorry I taped you. Despite what you may think, I *did* trust you. I just wanted to know more about you. I could have handled anything, Diego, *anything,* because—"

She pressed a shaking hand to her mouth, stopping the words. She jerked the door handle and pushed herself out of the car.

He leaned across the seat. "I should come up with you, check things—"

"Your responsibilities have ended, honey. Now, don't you be worryin' none about me. Brendan would remind us of Shakespeare's immortal words. 'Hasty marriage seldom proveth well.' Guess we never stood a chance, huh? *Adios,* Zorro."

The shrill wail of her security alarm pierced the wall of stoicism she'd retreated behind. She punched in the code, then pounded the wall beside the panel, wishing she could rip it out.

She let the anger come first, a powerful tornado that swept up the floating debris of regret, rejection and loss. The storm sucked it into the dark whirlwind, leaving behind only the joy. The moments of wonder. The laughter. The friendship. The love.

She reached for the shimmering light of love that was left when everything else swirled away.

Needing him, she went into his bedroom, dragged his pillow up and hugged it to her. His scent clung to the fabric, the scent that had brought her peace when he'd held her close, the scent that had made her body quiver and her heart soar.

"I wish I'd never met you."

His words wrenched a sob from her, just as his fever had freed the truth from him.

Now she had to find a way to live with it.

Fourteen

———

"**I** saw your bedroom light on," J.D. said to his father as he was welcomed into Duncan's house a week later. "I hope it's not too late to stop by."

"Not at all. Misty will join us in a minute, if you don't mind. She's making herself presentable."

They walked in tandem down the hall, heading by habit for Duncan's den. "If I'm interrupting something—"

"You are. But that's all right. We were married night before last."

Grinning, J.D. pounded him on the back. "Well, hallelujah! I can't think of better news to come home to. It took you long enough."

The judge scratched his head, a lopsided grin taking ten years off him. "We would have held off for you to be best man, but after waiting so many years for her I wasn't taking any chances she'd change her mind."

"He's lying," Misty said as she breezed into the room. "I

was the one who was worried. I'm still pinching myself. Hello, J.D. Welcome home."

"Mrs. Shaunnessey," J.D. said after he hugged her. "Welcome to the family."

"I can't believe I didn't figure out your connection to Duncan. I guess because you don't look like a Jimmy, which is all he ever calls you," Misty said, glancing from one to the other. "Now that I know, I can see the resemblance, in looks as well as pigheaded obstinance."

"Well. I feel complimented. How about you, Dad?"

Duncan smiled. "How was Florida, son?"

"Six days of sunshine that I saw from inside a building. I couldn't wait to get back to Fog City so I wouldn't feel so deprived."

"Looks like you have a solid case, Jimmy," the judge said. "You did a good job."

"The list of charges grows daily. It's been gratifying."

"Have you seen Maggie?" Misty asked.

J.D. picked up a letter opener from the desk and toyed with it. "I just got home."

"And you came *here* first?"

"My love, please—"

"Stay out of this, Duncan. You told me yourself he was the biggest fool alive."

Duncan offered his son a sheepish grin in apology as she turned back to J.D.

"I've got Maggie busy developing a new line for my company," Misty announced. "Moonlight and Magnolias. I haven't told her the name yet. I hope she'll be pleased."

"That's great," J.D. said, stabbing the letter opener into an envelope lying on the desktop. "Great. Now all she needs is a husband, a handful of kids and the white picket fence."

"Seems to me she had the husband part of it." Duncan plucked the weapon away, rescuing his correspondence from further wounding. "Go see her, son. Ask her if that's what she wants."

"She already told me. She was moved around a lot as a

child. She wants to live in the same house forever, for her children to have the stability she never had. You know if I want to advance in the Bureau, I will probably be transferred several times."

It was the reason he hadn't ever let himself imagine a permanent life with her. He couldn't give her what she wanted, what she deserved.

A succinct expletive shattered his self-pity. Misty, hands on hips, advanced on him. "You're an idiot."

She wasn't calling him anything he hadn't called himself. He'd done nothing but think about Magnolia for the past week, worried if she was all right, wondered if she was pregnant.

Hoped that she was pregnant. There would be no decision to make if that were true. She would marry him. Period.

"Almost twenty-five years ago," Misty said, grabbing his arm and turning him to face her, "your father defended me on solicitation charges. It was the lowest point of my life. I'd run away from an abusive husband. No one would give me a job. There weren't shelters available as there are now. I was a mess. But I swear I never attempted to sell my body. However, some streetwalkers had taken me under their wing, seeing a fellow victim, and I got caught up with them in a police sweep one night."

She reached out to her husband, who came to her side instantly.

"Duncan saw past my bruises and my scars, even the invisible ones. He was the kindest, gentlest man I'd ever known. I didn't believe he could be real. I figured it was just a tactic I hadn't been exposed to before. Kill 'em with kindness or something. He got the charges dropped, helped me divorce my husband, found me a respectable job. Then when my life settled down, he came calling.

"I put him off. I let him be my friend and occasionally my lover for all these years. But I wouldn't let him into my heart. Then you and Maggie got married. Day in and day out I saw her happiness, and it hit me, how foolish I'd been to have denied myself that same joy. It was my fault alone, but it wasn't only *my* loss. Because I would never cut Duncan free completely, he hadn't moved on with his life."

"You don't have to do this, my love," Duncan said, pressing a kiss to her temple.

"If I can atone in some way through your son, I'm going to," she said fiercely. "Maggie's trying so hard to put on a happy face for everyone, but all of us who love her see the truth. She's making herself sick with blame."

J.D.'s heart turned over. "She is ill?"

"Go see her," Misty said quietly. "Settle this. Either make her yours completely and forever—or set her free. You both deserve that."

He took her hand in his, pausing for a moment to get his bearings again. "A week of soul-searching had already led me to that conclusion. But thank you for your honesty. Mom."

Misty lifted one perfectly arched brow. "If you ever call me Mom again, hon, I'm going to cut you out of the will."

Her lights were on. Even though she'd gotten off work at midnight, she was still up now, an hour later.

He should have called first. Having someone knock on her door at this hour was bound to frighten her. His cellular phone was in the glove compartment. He considered using it, shrugged, then climbed out of the car.

When he reached the top of her stairs, he blew out a breath, straightened his sweater and knocked on her door. Seconds ticked into aeons.

"Who is it?" Her tone was no-nonsense, her voice strong.

"Diego." *Diego.* He'd never called himself by the name she always used, yet it had come automatically, comfortably.

"What do you want?"

Huh? "I want to see you, Magnolia. Please open the door."

"We agreed on three weeks."

What the hell? "So, I'm early. Don't make me stand out here and yell. Someone will call the police."

"A deal's a deal. Go away."

He smiled at the belligerence in her voice. "I have my key. I know the code."

"I changed it."

"No, you didn't. You told me I could come get my things. You wouldn't have changed it until after I'd done that."

A moment of silence passed, then, "Are you here for your stuff?"

"Would it be too much trouble?"

After a minute he heard the click of the lock.

"Come in," she called.

He stepped in cautiously, closing the door behind him. She was nowhere in sight.

"I boxed up almost everything," she called from her bedroom. "You can start carrying it to your car. I've just got a couple more things to get."

He glanced at the cartons stacked neatly beside her computer. "Can't you even look at me, Magnolia?" he called back.

She stepped through the doorway and his heart turned cartwheels up his throat, halting his ability to speak, as the truth burst from him in an explosive jolt. He was in love with her. Somewhere along the way, he'd fallen deeply, irrevocably in love with her.

"Hi," he said finally.

She looked at him with huge, serious eyes. She didn't move, but he could see her shrug her armor on.

"How are you?" she asked politely.

"Not so good."

Bewildered, Maggie frowned. What was he doing here? What kind of new torture did he have in mind? "Your jacket is in the closet. Here, take this, too."

She passed him a long, narrow box.

"The pearl necklace you gave me." She grabbed his grandmother's rings and twisted them up her finger. *Please, God, let me get through this without crying. Please.*

"Don't take them off." His hand curled around her wrist, stopping her. His left hand. The wedding ring she'd given him gleamed as she pushed her rings back in place. She lifted her gaze slowly. What did it mean? What—

He framed her face with his hands. His eyes glittered darkly, then softened to liquid chocolate. "I missed you, Magnolia."

A moan tumbled from her before she could catch it. She clamped his wrists, holding on as she felt her resolve crumble.

"I missed you too," she whispered, her heart pounding. "Oh, Diego, I missed you so much. So very, very much."

He brushed his lips across hers gently, a light drag of flesh to flesh, tentative, searching, questioning. He breathed her name again and again until she clung to him, calling out his. He lifted her in his arms.

"You have lost weight. You have not been taking care of yourself." His voice was gruff and oh, so dear.

"It doesn't matter." She pressed her lips to his neck, twining her arms around him as he laid her on the bed, pulling him down with her, making him her blanket, her comforter. Still, she shivered in anticipation.

She knew she should wait for the words from him. The right words. Or maybe she should say them first. "Diego—"

"Shh. We'll talk later. For now I just want to hold you, and feel you quiver, and hear your sighs of pleasure. I feel as if I've waited my whole life for this moment."

His mouth came down on hers. His tongue slid across her lips, dipped inside as she opened to him, and mated with hers. A primal sound vibrated from his chest to hers. She sucked in a breath and wrapped her legs around him as he moved against her, pressing kisses to her temples, her eyelids, her cheeks, and finally her mouth again.

Needing to be free of restriction, he whipped his clothes off between hungry kisses, then forced himself to slow down, to make a memory of the moment. He stretched out beside her, leaning across her to turn on the small lamp beside her bed.

"You are so beautiful," he said, the words burning his throat with their truth.

"Diego," she whispered.

He pushed her sweatshirt over her head and shoved it across

the bed. Brushing a satin bra strap aside, he kissed the smooth
flesh of her shoulder and tugged the strap lower and lower,
until he'd peeled the lace away from her breast so he could
look at her.

"Please," she moaned.

He ran his thumb over the hard nipple, shifting his gaze to
her face as she arched, moaned and closed her eyes. She
arched higher, holding her breath when he tasted her, sweeping
the peak with his tongue, stroking the underside.

"I want you," she pleaded.

He pulled the crest into his mouth, flicking the catch of her
bra open to bare her other breast, reveling in the way she
pushed herself toward him, celebrating the sounds she made.

Her words were little more than a growl. "I need you."

An inch at a time, he unwrapped her, until all that was left
were lacy panties. He angled up to slide the piece of temptation off her, then he balled the fabric and brushed her body
with it in long, steady strokes. She gasped as the lace scraped
her nipples.

"I—"

"Shh. Let me take care of you, *novia.*"

He left a trail of fire with his tongue as he loved her. There
was nothing she could say, nothing she could do but savor it.
And when he found her most sensitive spot, he cherished her
until she cried out. Then he was inside her, stretching her,
filling her, taking her up again fast and hard until she slammed
into the climax that waited at the top. He kept moving, slowly,
steadily, wondrously. She didn't think she could possibly...

But she did, journeying with him, finding the pleasure together, treasuring the beauty, wondering at the need that stayed
beyond fulfillment. She would never be satisfied, never have
her fill of him.

He held himself off her slightly, found the rhythm of
breathing again, heard her find her own. He smiled as she
sighed loudly. Ah, but there was such pleasure here, such contentment, such endless joy.

He rolled to his side and rested a hand on her abdomen,

moving his thumb up and down, stroking the hollow of her belly and the padded jut of hipbone.

"Do you think you're pregnant?"

He watched her stiffen.

"Magnolia?"

She shoved his hand off her and rolled away. "Get out of my bed. Get out of my life."

"What? Why?" He sat up, bewildered, automatically reaching for his jeans and pulling them on as she disappeared into the bathroom. When she emerged, she was bundled in a robe.

"I said get out."

"What did I do? I thought you wanted that as much as I did."

"I thought you came here because you missed me," she said, breathing hard. "Now I find it's only because you want to know if I'm pregnant."

"That's not—"

"Well, here's a news flash for you, Zorro. I'm on the Pill. I've been on the Pill since two weeks after we met. I'm not pregnant, so don't worry about that. Now, get out of my house."

He shoved his hands in his pockets. "You did not want my child?"

"Are you always this dense, or is it just with me?" She threw up her hands and stalked away.

He followed her into the living room, where she stormed around the room. He tried to control his temper. "I do not understand."

"I was on the Pill because I didn't want to trap you," she shouted. "I have no idea how I can continue to love you when you offer me nothing in return except obligation and macho attitude. But I'll tell you this, James Diego Shaunnessey, I'm sure I can stop loving you as soon as you're gone from my life. So get out. I want to be sane again."

"You love me?" he asked quietly.

"Of course I love you. What do you think that—" she gestured wildly toward the bedroom "—was all about?"

"I love you too."

"How can you be so— What?"

He took advantage of her stillness to approach her. "I love you, Magnolia."

Maggie swallowed hard. "You said you wished you'd never met me."

He frowned. "When?"

"In your fever. When I taped you."

"I don't think you can hold me responsible for what I said in a fever, *novia*. But it isn't how I felt—or how I feel. What I resented was how knowing you had forced me to re-examine my life. My dreams. I'm not comfortable looking that deeply into myself." He pulled her into his arms and held her, tucking her head under his chin. "You turned my world upside down. I didn't know how to handle it. All I could see was the job I had to do. And you kept getting in the way."

He tightened his hold on her. "I fell in love with you anyway. I think in some way I was waiting to hear the words from you first. I was afraid if I let myself acknowledge how I felt it would leave me too vulnerable. Like my father had been. I was afraid you'd leave me. I'm still afraid of that."

She burrowed closer, her heart full. "I promise I won't ever leave you. Ever."

"I want to marry you."

She leaned back at the hesitance in his voice. "But?"

He brushed his hand down her hair over and over. "I like my job."

"Of course you do."

"I know it's not cool to say this out loud, but I love my country. I believe in truth and justice and the American way."

"Well, good. So do I. But what's that got to do with anything?"

"I can't guarantee you one house, one place to raise our children. Promotions often mean relocation. And I expect to climb the ladder."

"All right."

"You'd probably just get the house the way you like it or the kids settled in school when I'll be transferred again."

"And I'll pack up the house and arrange for a mover and off we'll go. What's the problem?"

"You said you wanted your children to have stability. A sense of place. I can't guarantee that."

"I also said I was building a career at home so that I could be there with them. That's stability." She rested her hands on his chest. "Don't you see? It's precisely because I'm a homebody that this can work for us. I can create a home anywhere. All that matters is that we share a life together."

"You won't regret it later?"

"Diego. I love you. I loved you when you took care of me, spoiled me and worried about me. I also loved you when you ignored, rejected and ordered me. Love's like that. It won't be easy all the time. But the love's not going to change, except to deepen. Home is wherever you are."

He brushed her hair back, left his hands there to frame her face. "Then I think the first order of business should be another wedding."

The most gloriously sexy shimmer settled in her eyes as she drew a leisurely Z across his chest. His heart slammed into his sternum, jump-starting desire again.

"I have this spectacular red teddy, Zorro, that I've been keeping in perfumed tissue paper since my birthday."

He let his imagination lock in the image before he kissed her, thoroughly, possessively, dangerously, dragging her closer and closer.

"Then again," he said against her lips, "I think tomorrow might be a better day to plan a wedding."

"And a lifetime."

He held her near to his heart and closed his eyes. "And a lifetime," he agreed softly.

*   *   *   *   *

In the tradition of
Anne Rice comes a
daring, darkly sensual
vampire novel by

MAGGIE SHAYNE

BORN IN TWILIGHT

Rendezvous hails bestselling Maggie Shayne's vampire
romance series, WINGS IN THE NIGHT, as
"powerful...riveting...unique...intensely romantic."

Don't miss it, this March, available
wherever Silhouette books are sold.

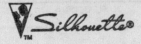

Take 4 bestselling love stories FREE

Plus get a FREE surprise gift!

As seen on TV!
Free Gift Offer

With a Free Gift proof-of-purchase from any Silhouette® book,
you can receive a beautiful cubic zirconia pendant.

This gorgeous marquise-shaped stone is a genuine cubic
zirconia—accented by an 18" gold tone necklace.
(Approximate retail value $19.95)

Send for yours today...
compliments of ▽ *Silhouette®*
TM

To receive your free gift, a cubic zirconia pendant, send us one original proof-of-purchase, photocopies not accepted, from the back of any Silhouette Romance™, Silhouette Desire®, Silhouette Special Edition®, Silhouette Intimate Moments® or Silhouette Yours Truly™ title available in February, March and April at your favorite retail outlet, together with the Free Gift Certificate, plus a check or money order for $1.65 U.S./$2.15 CAN. (do not send cash) to cover postage and handling, payable to Silhouette Free Gift Offer. We will send you the specified gift. Allow 6 to 8 weeks for delivery. Offer good until April 30, 1997 or while quantities last. Offer valid in the U.S. and Canada only.

Free Gift Certificate

Name: _____

Address: _____

City: _____ State/Province: _____ Zip/Postal Code: _____

Mail this certificate, one proof-of-purchase and a check or money order for postage and handling to: SILHOUETTE FREE GIFT OFFER 1997. In the U.S.: 3010 Walden Avenue, P.O. Box 9077, Buffalo NY 14269-9077. In Canada: P.O. Box 613, Fort Erie, Ontario L2Z 5X3.

FREE GIFT OFFER   084-KFD

ONE PROOF-OF-PURCHASE

To collect your fabulous FREE GIFT, a cubic zirconia pendant, you must include this original proof-of-purchase for each gift with the properly completed Free Gift Certificate.

084-KFD

Beginning next month from

SILHOUETTE®

Desire

by
Elizabeth Bevarly

Watch as three siblings separated in childhood
are reunited and find love along the way!

ROXY AND THE RICH MAN (D #1053, February 1997)—
Wealthy businessman Spencer Melbourne finds love with the
sexy female detective he hires to find his long-lost twin.

LUCY AND THE LONER (D #1063, April 1997)—
Independent Lucy Dolan shows her gratitude to the fire
fighter who comes to her rescue—by becoming his slave
for a month.

And coming your way in July 1997—
THE FAMILY McCORMICK continues with the wonderful
story of the oldest McCormick sibling. Don't miss any of
these delightful stories. Only from Silhouette Desire.

You're About to Become a *Privileged Woman*

Reap the rewards of fabulous free gifts and benefits with proofs-of-purchase from Silhouette and Harlequin books

Pages & Privileges™

It's our way of thanking you for buying our books at your favorite retail stores.

PROOF OF PURCHASE

SD-PP23

Offer expires March 31, 1997

Harlequin and Silhouette— the most privileged readers in the world!

For more information about Harlequin and Silhouette's PAGES & PRIVILEGES program call the Pages & Privileges Benefits Desk: 1-503-794-2499

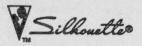

Silhouette®

SD-PP23